Adept

Book 2 of Sen of the Woods

Mab Morris

The full trilogy of Sen of the Woods
is dedicated to Alex Levy.
For all the years we explored the woods together!

Adept is dedicated to Laura Ownbey.
Without your Hard work, this book, this trilogy, could never have
become what it became!
Thank you for all the years of work we've done together.

Contents

Chapter One

The end of the month of the Apatin, the end of spring

Getting the adept symbol cut onto the top of my left hand did not hurt quite as much as having the sacred white clay rubbed into it. That stung more than I could imagine. The clay was necessary to give the Doctor-Diviner adept scar its distinctive coloring and raised shape. Tages had blessed the scar and wrapped it carefully for me. I'd have to redress the wound every day till it healed.

I watched him leave, with his bag full of bits from a Tree he could not see. I leaned against that Tree, thanking it for my good fortune. Some of the flowers fell upon my head. They smelled something like an apple blossom, yet with something both familiar and strange adding to its unworldly aroma. Behind me, on the far side of the Tree, I could almost hear ants crawling up and down it, chewing upon the rot like termites. A whiffle of sound caught my attention as some rot fell off the Tree.

In my bag, I had part of a broken necklace said to once have belonged to the Goddess Thielle. I didn't open my bag to look at it, and hadn't shown it to Tages before he'd left. I'd only found it a few days before in Grandmother Turani's home. I wanted to understand why she might have had it. It mattered. There was another larger part in the lord of Thefarland's treasure room. It had been the source of much conflict.

Lord Aranthur, to the north, had wanted it as part of a wedding price, and had convinced the father of his future daughter-in-law to ask for it in exchange for her valuable property of the Westvell. Thefare's brother, Fuluns, had scuppered not only the negotiations but the marriage by raping that young girl, Ravantha.

Aranthur was still vying for it as a magical relic that might heal him, when Zelia and Tages—the last of the respected Doctor-Diviners—couldn't. Tages didn't think modern science would heal him, either. I suspected Aranthur's son, Marce, Ravantha's former intended, was cursed with the same ailment he had.

It was disconcerting to have that bit of bauble in my bag that few even knew about.

To comfort myself, I sang the lullaby Grandmother Turani had sung to me as a child, one that I believe about finding me after my parents had left me to die of exposure. At least what I could remember of the song. More of it had come back to me in the past few weeks.

> *"One was wrapped*
> *In lace and gold*
> *Another leaves and dirt*
> *One died in the cold*
> *The other death did skirt*
>
> *One was lost, another lives*

Oh, the humble child
Into my arms did come"

A few words continued trying to finish other lines, words like wild or drum, and even bum... but they continued to be increasingly improbable, and sometimes silly enough to make me laugh. Still, I hummed the lines and let myself remember Grandmother Turani's safe embrace. Warmed by the sunlight and the Tree's strange comfort, and looking again at my wrapped left hand, I was content again.

I breathed in the smell of the blossoms and the sweet smell of the Tree's dying. A Tree in constant transition between life and death. Here I was at yet another beginning of my own, again at the base of this Tree.

Not too long ago, Tages wouldn't give me the elevation to adept status. During a ceremony earlier that spring, I was not able to see any of my own ancestors. I had seen two goddesses, and this Tree, but none of my own deceased people. It was necessary for our work. While we used nature in much of our healing and our Medicine, we also used ancestors—for they might cause illnesses if they felt any disrespect. In any community we worked with, we often called upon members who had already been healed as minor doctors, proof that healing was possible, bringing to light any disruption that harmed. This extended to the afterlife.

I still wondered if leaving me to die by this Tree had cut me off from all ancestors. This was, I knew, where Grandmother Turani had found me. No matter.

Finding me here, Tages had discovered that the Tree I'd drawn, whose flowers I'd brought back and he'd held in his own astonished hands—flowers he'd never seen in his entire life— proved how much I could see and he could not, even while standing under its branches. He changed his mind.

All this bemused me. Tages was one of the greatest Doctor-Diviners in the country, and possibly in history. It was, however, a dying profession. There were too many changes in the world. Science was easily outstripping most of the charlatans who claimed the title of Doctor-Diviner, singing nonsense, and dancing to rhythms that had no Medicine.

Neither Tages nor I could regret science emerging as a beneficial healing art—except it had no Medicine, no community, no... well... anything divine about it.

Even Tage's son, Aule, had left for the city of Jambrone to study at the university. He *could* not see the other world—ancestors or otherwise. He could see much in the fields of chemistry and biology. These studies his father and I embraced and took note of. Even my work using the taxonomy from biology and botany had become useful in creating a comparative dictionary of the ancient lore-laden Ndeb. Tages had finally read the work I'd been doing and approved. He suggested that this would be worthy adept work, as well as being allowed to practice our craft farther afield to tend the villages he had been neglecting of late.

While slowly making my way home, I spent some time gathering herbs for the garden, as well as for study. I had to be careful, one-handed as I was. Each day, I cleaned the wound on my hand, purifying it with white clay.

Jackal, the jackal of all jackals, often walked with me. He seemed all too amused by something, laughing with Crow, who flew silently through the woods with us. Some of the time, she flew with a flock, all silent as death, and then the murder would suddenly caw at me as a group from some unexpected part of the woods came along our path. Crow, flying low and nearly perching on Jackal's back, laughed at how startled I might be.

Once, as I sat by a stream, trying to catch fish for my dinner —Jackal grinning at my lack of luck, but not helping either—Crow dropped an apple on my head. It smelled of that mystical Tree's blossoms. The juice bled from where its claws had held it.

"Thank you!" I cried out, but wasn't sure I should eat it. It was fresh, and it was still too early in the season for such fruit.

She only cawed at me, with derisive laughter.

"She'll learn," called out Jackal, "with both of us teaching her!" But he was just as mocking as the cawing from above.

Learn what? I wondered. But if Jackal wouldn't tell me, I doubted Crow would, either.

Book of Summer

Chapter Two

The month of Aritimi, early summer

I arrived home on the first day of Aritimi. I got straight to work. I took a flower press I'd left there before my last dreadful trip to Ravantha and checked it. Apparently, Tages had built fires in the room to keep it and all our equipment dry. He'd turned my hut more into a laboratory than my sleeping chambers. I could see that he'd set up equipment for extracts as well as essential oils. I sighed.

Well, I had long been used to sleeping in his laboratory. *This one is at least partly mine*, I thought, wondering where I'd put my bed. Currently, it was partly under a table. I looked at my left hand and smiled.

The plants in either press had not turned to mold, which was a relief. I put both presses aside and carefully rearranged the space so I would have a place to sleep without hitting my head or knocking anything aside if I slept restless or woke in the dark of night.

I rearranged the laboratory so I could work on one of the

tables. I needed to put the pressed flowers behind good paper and precious glass to better draw and study them. I had taken good notes, but I was further glad of a good memory.

Pressing a flower sometimes would take all the color out, depending on the age of the pressed plant. They also flattened the beautiful curl of their corolla. New words for me. Corolla, the inner whorl of the perianth, that puts its face toward the sun. The corolla, surrounding pistils and stamens. The perianth's display of color that would attract pollinators of bees, butterflies, and even small birds.

I carefully drew the Nighee, thinking of its scientific name, *Borreenus giren*. There were similar plants, but not local. Tages said one variation of the Nighee grew in the rockier slopes and was smellier. The other could be found near Zelia's region to the north. She'd told him it branched out more and was more potent, thus more dangerous. She'd sent a supply, just as we sent her some of the medicinal herbs she could not easily find in her area.

I drew the Nighee as it might be seen in life, but used the pressed plants to gather the information that would help classify it using the new botanical taxonomy. As I drew, I thought, *It's so very pretty, and the flowers so delicate.*

However, dark green made it a plant in the black side of the Ndeb plant taxonomy, though the flowers were white. Death and grace, of course. But the new taxonomy would have the dark green, leathery leaves numbered according to how it was palmately parted, among other characteristics. An interesting way to classify a plant—by traits, not by what it could do. In Ndeb, the plant was black and white, which meant dangerous, but potentially useful. Granted, the others variations of this plant were still green, so still black, and the flowers stank, signifying what we might call deceitful. I made notes about them, so I could paint them in at some later date, and try to find a way to reconcile the two very different ways of classifying a plant.

How would I organize the future book so that it could be useful? The Nighee was a good example of how challenging a chore it might become, but exciting to me, nonetheless.

The work of drawing and note-taking was necessary to free up the presses. I would need both skills on my upcoming travels. I also needed to carefully write down my notes about the plants I had just gathered.

I also made notes of plants I wanted to gather or draw, checking in on the garden to see what had survived transplanting, as well as our medicine stores to see what roots, bark, or berries I needed to gather. Some fruit bushes would begin bearing early, with more coming as the sun plumped the produce after all this rain, building toward abundance in autumn.

I tried to visit with Hastia, as she was now among those I might consider a friend, the first female one, but she was too busy being a woman now. And soon to be a wife? It seemed so. There would be no commiserating about my elevation. Despite our similar ages, I hadn't had a three-day-long Milk Tree ceremony. I hadn't been initiated into womanhood. In her eyes, it seemed, I was just a girl and always would be.

The next month would be less wet from all of the Apatin's rains, and travel would be much easier. During the few days of preparation, Tages would come in and review his own mental map of the area and help me build my own. There were places he wanted me to visit that he would not be going to see any time soon, unless at need, if the healing or divining was beyond me.

Tricky this, as divination was becoming weak in him, an

unwelcome admission. He hoped that what I *could* see, and others couldn't, might build a new or different practice of divination so important to our work. It would help both of us. Tages was eager to traverse new mystical ground in his studies, along with what he could gain from his son, and the doctors from the university he corresponded with.

Yet he was sending me away before that study could even begin.

Traveling from village to village in the month of Aritimi was somewhat dangerous. Not for the usual issues of lions and jackals looking for food, but because it was a time for men to take young hunters out for the first time to hunt fowl for food. The arrows they learned with might not kill you, except by freakish chance, but their aim was often wild, and sometimes it took hard lessons for them to learn to aim their bows carefully.

My travels showed anew how old ways were diminishing, but also that tensions were growing along the Westvell and Thefarland borders. In spring, my time in the Westvell, the tensions were mine alone. Now I observed more. A community... two communities with a growing diss-ease I knew Tages needed to know about.

I was in Fareli, close to the Westvell border, having salved a scrape and bruise from a boy who hadn't learned yet to steady his bow. The mother was a little too protective and had interfered, though the boy's father had already used some wild herbs to ease the wound. No wonder the boys' initiation rituals were done far away from a mother's attention.

The local midwife found me just as I was packing up to leave.

"I am Thesathei. You're a student of Tages. You know Velia?"

"Yes, of course I know her."

"There's a girl, married, no Milk Tree. I might want your help. The labor is taking too long. I am worried. She's so young."

Velia had, of course, spoken of midwifery many times. The whole household heartily agreed with her that the Milk Tree ceremony was important, for it was only performed when the girl's body could support a baby's growth. Womanhood was the result of the initiation, and marriage often afterward. Much of what Velia discussed about midwifery and women's rituals, even when Tages considered helping her as part of our practice, was entirely theoretical. "I'm not..." I began.

"Come," Thesathei interrupted. "There are already minor doctors dancing for Vesi, but none labored so long, or while so young."

I nodded. This *was* part of my adept work. Theory and observation turned into practice. Tages should have accompanied me on my first trip out, but I steadied my nerves with one last shake and followed, hoisting my bags onto my back. It hopefully meant that he trusted me.

I began to note that how little Tages might divine, his knowledge of the area remained profound. I did have herbs and rootstock for occasions like this. My bag was prepared for anything I would see.

The girl—for surely she still was wife and mother, regardless —was struggling out of pure exhaustion. Thesathei had listed all the herbs she'd given the poor thing on our short walk. At this point, they were too gentle. Apparently, her body was not dilating enough to birth.

"I have the rootstock of belit," I said.

"Is that not dangerous?"

"We certainly should not give her too much. A weak dose for this mother, in fact, but..." I felt a little helpless and a bit of a fraud, except through my observations and a flood of memories discussing a case like this, it came to me. "She cannot wait much longer, can she? You said it has been days?" I asked, but I could see it clearly in the room.

Thesathei nodded.

"Even her minor doctors are tired," I said. "We will be careful. There might be tearing."

"With this child, there would be tearing anyway," Thesathei admitted. "You will help stitch her up? The baby will need my care as it is a difficult journey for it as well."

"Of course."

I brewed the root, and my mind began its usual litany of thought. I thought of how the belit was classified in Ndeb as an *assisting* plant. I wondered about the taxonomy it would have in the modern science, stripped of its usefulness to mere appearance. I brought out some herbs that fortified, something for the body that wasn't merely Medicine, and had one of the exhausted dancers brew the tea and make a stew. The broth would be useful to the girl.

"In my day," whispered the dancer, "the man would come to his wife's hut. Here, even her ancestors do not know her husband's family."

"How, then, did they meet?" I asked.

"At the Grand Market by the castle. Vesi is pretty, and the family poor. Tcha gave the family a cow, and they could not pass that up, even though the cow should have been hers. They kept it to help feed their family."

"That is shocking," I said in full agreement.

The brew was finished, and I went to give it to the girl. She took it in slow sips between contractions. Between this decoction and the broth from the stew, she began to revive. The belit did assist, and the dancers began to dance, slow and steady, singing quietly to gentle the girl's struggles. I was grateful for Thesathei and her competence. Noting the increased dilation with her fingers, she gave helpful encouragement to the girl.

When the baby came, it was blue and needed care. She took it toward the fire and rubbed it, having one of the minor doctors cut the umbilical cord. The baby cried out, finally, while I waited for the afterbirth and ensured that the entire placenta was out. This still took time, and I was glad the belit helped the contractions continue till this was done. I then cleaned the area of blood and sewed the tear up.

When the baby had fed and the new mother slept, Thesathei and I watched for more bleeding and anything else that might happen.

"I'll be sending a note to Tages. I'll write Velia, as well, in case of a fistula. She's young, and the birth was difficult," I said. "Unless you know how to..."

"No, I'd need her help. That's something too deep inside and would need Velia's great care. Thank you."

I'd already written the note. Ndeb for Tages, and Obrone for Velia. In the morning, I'd hand it to someone going to the market or to town.

There was a banging at the door, and when opened by a furious Thesathei, muttering about impatient husbands, she was surprised when a man bowed to her. He was, I could see, someone she did not know, and she was frightened. She used a word I'd not heard before, cursing him as a foreigner and a Westvellian.

"I offer no harm!" he said, but his tone was resentful. "Please. We understood that the Doctor-Diviner was here, the adept. We need help with an eye. The adept is here?"

"I am," I said and began to put my things in my bags.

"Please come. He is a tinker traveling through the Westvell, and he... he went too near a field where the boys practiced."

I finished packing and gave Thesathei the note. "Please have it sent to Tages and Velia as soon as possible."

She nodded and I left. I couldn't help but think that an eye was not as important as the girl, but I knew she would do well, and if needing any further care, Thesathei was capable, and Velia was much better than I with that sort of thing.

I was still irritated by having to leave. His conversation did not help. "You should not be used for such things. They've a midwife in their village. You're an adept and the Westvell needs you. Ravantha would claim you as our Doctor-Diviner. You should be with us, not them, no matter where you've studied."

I doubted this. Ravantha considered Tages a glorified apothecary.

"I'm coming, aren't I? And Tages has long cared for people in the Westvell. Cai is a Master Doctor-Diviner and takes care of your people closer to Rasce's lands."

"Let them care for Rascenden and Thefarland. You are ours."

"That girl needed a Doctor-Diviner," I said. A half-truth. If Velia was not available, then I stood a close second, or rather third.

The irritation only continued as the man and I walked. He seemed to relax only when we crossed the border. Then, the patient only added to my frustration. The man had not cleaned his minor wound. It had gotten infected while he rested in the village as an apology for the injury. Normally, he'd have been escorted out as soon as his work there was done. Strangers, especially men, weren't suffered to stay long in the Westvell.

The arrows for fowl weren't large and weren't barbed, either. The glancing blow at the corner of the man's eye was swollen, and the small gash, definitely infected. I gave him a sedative, numbed the area with a salve, and got to work. I released the infection to reduce the swelling. I added a poultice wrapped in a cloth to help draw out any infecting dirt that might still be in the wound. A waiting game. It gave me time to think.

For one, however much the villagers might want to claim me as their Doctor-Diviner, I was from Thefarland and their hospitality was grudging.

For the most part, Tages and I did not tend to minor Hunter Cult training wounds. Even before I'd started my apprenticeship with Tages, I'd known Kutu—one of my first friends, and a respected leader and hunter. Grandmother Turani had given his cult, and others, herbs and advice to heal minor injuries. Immediate first aid was often important when far from any reputable healer.

I lifted the poultice and irrigated the tinker's wound to remove the tinier particulates that might have entered the small gash. The sedative worked well enough to where the only distraction was his snores. My mind wandered again.

The month of young hunters seemed misnamed to me. Aritimi was a woman.

Depending on the lore or legend, she was a heroine or Goddess of the Hunt, so it never made sense to me to name the month for a time when rambunctious boys learned to hunt fowl. It was also one of the months for initiating young boys. Celi was another.

The only women hunters I encountered were closer to the Westvell, where Ravantha had initiated a growing number of women into her own Hunter Cult—if that was what anyone could call it. As far as I could tell, there was no initiation, only a will to hunt and practice. I had wondered how the men felt about their activities, but from what I could see, they did not mind, for the most part. Not in the Westvell, at any rate.

What would have surprised a good many of Thefare's men, including my friend Kutu in the Westvell, was that there were men who preferred farming. Those few villagers, including men, I'd spoken to on my rounds seemed to indicate that they were mainly preparing to defend their borders. Women who hunted gave more time for the men to practice the harder sports of fighting, often left only to men with far more wealth.

I irrigated the wound a few more times, peeked in with my second sight to note that the wound was as clean as I could get it. I considered a stitch for the small gash, but the man seemed eager to make a scene, so I put a bandage next to his eye, and then wrapped his head in another bandage to keep it there.

Then I left the village to venture toward the next. Gathering plants along the way gave me much time to ponder the evidence of the town's tensions.

Adept

Ravantha's Aranthenvellian friends, Larce and Marce, had been teaching her to fight, as well as some of her women, people who are not traditionally allowed or able to learn those crafts. I wondered if Ravantha was creating an army. She certainly had women who were magnificent archers and men who could fight with trained noblemen. It was something I certainly had to let Tages know if he had not yet divined it.

After my talk with Tages at Jammon's ancient temple, I speculated that the two men might be manipulating Ravantha. I could not imagine who else might be fueling her anger or impulsive and irrational outbursts.

Tages and I had speculated that Ravantha's brain injury made emotional balance difficult for her. He accepted that I would not be the one to help heal her. I had doubts she'd let Tages attempt to help her as well—since she considered him a glorified apothecary—insulting me in the same breath she wanted to try and protect me as her precious long-lost daughter.

Without going deep into the Westvell, nearer Ravantha's ready embrace, I observed and took notes. As best I could, I removed all of my opinions from the symptoms observed.

The land was showing signs of disease that were only seen in ways that had little to do with the physical health of the landscape or people.

I had to admit that the general populace seemed largely content and friendly. Most of the villages were prosperous. Exercise surely was healthy. There was a brisk export of grain, but little import of beef, fresh or cured. The cloth women wore on special days was locally woven and exquisitely embroidered. For the wealthiest in the villages and towns, the exotic foods rarely came from farther away than Thefarland towns. There were tins of

Yezginy teas that I'd tasted in Ravantha's own kitchens. Green, warm, and tasty. I always accepted a cup when offered in these houses.

The women were rather more fit than those in Thefarland. I observed that there was a readiness to fight. Once, in a village near a through-road, a merchant from Rascenden, on his way to the coast, was waylaid because of a shoe.

The men were ready to find offense—though none was offered. The poor man merely wanted to sleep in a good bed after a wearing journey and move on. He had sprung his shoes, and needed them to be sewn back together. I gave him poultices for his blisters. He felt uncomfortable, with reason.

I didn't get to hear the actual words. The villagers said nothing to me. They could not settle. They gathered in groups in the hall of the main house, where he'd grudgingly been allowed to stay. They whispered to each other, and one man or another, and sometimes women, would drift from one group to another, hands upon their weapons.

I didn't leave the man alone in such a tense atmosphere. In the morning, with the shoes repaired, we left. He thanked his hosts with deep and formal politeness. I guided him back to the main road myself and went toward the next village in my rounds.

Chapter Three

I discovered that I was given a pass to travel in the Westvell. I had thought it was my status as an adept Doctor-Diviner. It was not. Too many people assumed me to be Ravantha's daughter.

The further into the Westvell I went, the more passionately the villagers despised their eastern neighbors.

One plowman glared at me as if I were a stranger, and then patted me on my shoulder in commiseration that I had to work in Thefarland.

"They're thieves, stealing what they can from merchant trains from the coast," he said.

His wife, who gave me bread and honey, whispered, "They seduce their women, if not outright raping them. That's how they get their wives."

The stories they told were barely seeded in truth, and when I tried to heal the falsehood—as I was bound to do as a healer— they refused to hear me.

One burly woman named Cainei, in the village of Cisra, hated that I came from Thefarland. I was putting her shoulder joint back into place after a bad and ill-practiced wrestling match.

"You do not know—you have lived too long in Thefarland. They lie to you. They cheat you and are selfish. None of their people —except Tages and yourself—would ever show kindness to their neighbors! Their women have no thoughts in their heads for their own power, listening to men. They even did a Milk Tree ritual inside a man's home! How appalling is that, I ask you?"

I didn't let my frustration pass my lips. I'd seen more unkindness to strangers here than in Thefarland. I bit my lip and eased her away from the horror. Yet it was true. Hastia's Milk Tree ceremony had been done inside a man's home. Her uncle's. It was during the month of the Apatin. They'd have drowned in mud.

"Velia herself performed the ceremony," I said. "Surely you'd not doubt her ability or skill in Women's Arts?" It was a lucky shot, for as I said it, I knew Velia had tended Cainei during a very difficult birth. If she could show respect to Tages, then surely Tages's wife, who had helped her in great need, should be respected.

"She did?" Cainei asked, in some surprise. Her brows came together as she struggled to reconcile these disparate notions.

"Yes, and when so many young girls nowadays skip the tradition just to get married, surely this is something to celebrate!"

"Oh yes!" she said, and I could see her mind working against her ire.

I then exclaimed over some Thefarland bounty she had in her own home—I could not but recognize Velia's prized cheese, among other exotic items—to add to the healing of unreasonable resentments.

I could not understand this strange vehemence, even up against the crystal-clear proof of its reverse. I noticed it several times in my journeys. The weight of it grew.

It was beyond my ability to heal this sickness growing in the land. It needed far greater Medicine than I could provide on my own, and I was not at all sure what kind of minor doctors I could gather. It was a job for my master.

I was grateful to find my way back across the border, and at the first village, I sent a boy with another letter written entirely in Ndeb for Tages to read. I told him what I'd seen, but admitted I did not see any circumstances where the *fever* would erupt in full boil, only that I believed it could, given the right circumstances, or if not treated.

I didn't find the Thefarland countryside less problematic.

There weren't the whispers of rumors and resentment. There was less hate. There was a slight, but growing, concern about their neighbors across the border with whom they'd once traded amicably. If I'd met that resentment, I doubted these people would miss it. They did still trade with each other.

I could see the unmistakable Westvell weave in some of the fabrics they used for their clothes, and even their embroidered hems, vests, and ribbons.

Fortunately, there were disorders far more within my scope. Along the more northern border of the Westvell and Thefarland, I came across an illness inspired by a disgruntled ancestor. I could hear it wailing in the sick room. Finding minor doctors was easy enough for me. I looked for the subtle, spiritual marks on villagers that echoed in perhaps colors or waves—sometimes a strange tone—and that showed they also had experienced the same thing.

I painted the room with the sacred white clay, studied the patient, painted the minor doctors, and assured them that Tages had entrusted me with this Medicine. As it was clear I knew the old language, they did not quibble too much. They danced with a will, and I called the ancestor to notice how we were all dancing in sympathy for the patient's plight, and wanted it to release the patient from its grip.

Of course, I added herbs to the Medicine of dance and song, but the press of the ancestor's ire was strong. He was almost as clear to my eyes as the dancers.

I loved dances like this. They brought in former fellow sufferers of the same kinds of malady. They gave the patient a community that already understood the ailment, and did not blame them for neglect of an ancestor. They had erred the same way at least once before. It brought them all together for healing support as a community.

When the spirit was satiated, I dosed the patient with healing herbs. This time, we left the symbols on the walls as a reminder to the ancestors that we cared. I told them that after the patient had fully recovered for a week, they could wash the walls. Either I Tages or I would try to return in a few days to monitor the healing of the village.

Even as the sun grew in strength and the days in length, the growing gloom of it was thick, like a humid day. I could sense it as well as see it by signs I could observe. It made me wonder what could help heal a community inspired by hate.

I did not know. I wasn't sure what lore even Ndeb had and tried to think of lore or legends that might help. I yearned to talk with Tages as student to master. But as I was not yet home, and had work to do, I could think upon it. What would work?

A show of compassion or love? A revelation of a truth that showed that the time for hate was gone? The source was beyond my power—if my hypothesis was correct. What could I find to tell Ravantha that her revenge was of no purpose? She'd claimed me as a reason, as if a prize, and refused to budge from that reason. When I walked through parts of her land, I only fueled the truth of those rumors.

In another village, ten days later, there was another ancestor issue, but this one was of a young man's guilt for his own neglect. The ancestor, I believed, was long gone to another stage in the afterlife. I heard no wavering wail of sorrow from the other world. A ritual dance was arranged, but the symbols I drew were slightly different, and my words were for the young man who suffered. His participation was necessary. The herbs I gave were for nerves and hysteria.

Chapter Four

The most dangerous spirit I encountered was near the end of my travels in the village of Resala. A woman farmer named Nathaia had a bad rash, but clearly felt more than just itchy. She was somewhat unwell, and her heartbeat erratic, and her breath was uneven.

Jackal and Crow had joined me during my travels, but without saying much or doing much. But their presence had changed my eyes enough that I could see nature spirits, even where I did not expect them. Unlike the ancestor spirit, this was an earth spirit, that of a plant.

The flower had a red corolla, protecting pistil and stamen; it was haloed in white at the edges as the main petals curled out toward the sun. The base petals seemed to twirl down in strings of yellow, red, and white. It was, in truth, quite beautiful. And yet with all my studies in Ndeb, it was clearly in a poison arrow family, sometimes called Twisted Flower, or Twisted Rope, partly for the flower, as well as the vine. I had not seen this one yet.

The spirit, while it held its shape to a large extent, flickered like flame, being not quite in this world. Remembering the lessons from Jackal, I sat calmly and watched it. After a time, I knew I was more in its world than my own and could see and sense it more clearly. It showed me a great deal I had not known from my books. I knew its poison protected it from harm, and it could grow in wild patches in the woods. I had not known how easily it could spread, and that it could not only go beyond a topical irritation but also become systemic as well. No wonder it was a good poison arrow plant.

Then it went beyond that. Without my study of modern science, I doubt I would have understood. The portion of its makeup that caused irritation, extracted *very* carefully, could protect the heart. The diluted irritation entering the system, I gathered, was how it became beneficial. I could see the plant showing me this, see the tiny sparks of that component in its chemistry enter a body, and irritate… or rather inspire a sluggish heart to spark in response.

Too much, and I watched this *story*, too, and that sparking would make the heart beat erratically, and then all out of control.

I drew the plant for my journal, as well as the spirit plant, making notes on what it had told me. More, I took a sheet of paper and drew a copy of the plant for the farmer.

Apparently, she had cleared a field near a forest—trying to have more land to grow not only produce, but wheat and oats, with seeds she'd purchased from a surprisingly friendly Westvellian friend. She had secured a piece of land not wanted for cattle. Among many plants she had seen that would choke the field, or were inedible, was one plant she did not know was poisonous to the touch. No surprise. She wasn't a hunter. She'd never have a need for poison arrows.

While she had goats helping to clear the field, she had gone in with a will herself to help clear what the goats could not. She'd thrown it among the compost. I had, thankfully, read about similar plants in Tages's books and knew the antidote for those other variations. I gathered the slipper weed from the woods nearby. I first dosed the woman with the supplies I already had on hand, but showed her how to make more salve, as well as tea to help the more systemic parts of her irritations.

That done, I danced to banish the angry earth spirit—though we'd already spoken quite amicably—and its own aggravation from being damaged was already being forgiven.

Without touching the plant with my bare hands, I collected it with some waxed cloth the woman had given me and gathered it into my bag. I wanted to investigate its properties further, with its permission. I knew some of my hunter friends might like a potent weed like this for their work. I destroyed the compost to ensure that it had not sent out runners in the fertile waste to grow robustly and irritate or sicken yet more people. It caused a rash with physical contact, and more symptoms with deeper scratches from broken branches. It was surely dangerous if ingested. And some creatures had.

I did not need an echo of Jackal's voice to look further.

"Goat," I called out in Ndeb—hoping that a domesticated animal could still have a strong spirit animal. She came. And so quickly that my heart pounded.

"Will you help me see if any of your people ate this poison plant?"

Glad of my concern, she called them to her and helped me see the ones that would get ill or pass the poison to their milk.

"Is the same plant that I know of to heal my people the same that will heal yours?" I asked. It was.

The farmer thought I was a bit crazy to dose her goats, and at my orders that they should be carefully washed so that the oils of the plant would not rub off on her or any of her children who tended them.

"Perhaps I should ask Tages for advice," she said.

I was nettled by her words and gestured with my left hand, displaying my adept scarring.

"You can milk them," I said, "and feed poisoned milk to your family, by all means, if you do not trust that he's taught me well enough for him to send me out to villages to do the healing he's asked me to do." I tried hard not to have my annoyance go beyond my not-quite-passive words.

I really needed to learn not to react to perceived insults so rudely.

With a sigh, I realized that while I had done some Medicine, I had also been yet more mysterious than what she was entitled to expect. I had used lore that Jackal had taught me—something outside of my Doctor-Diviner work. Insight far beyond the tossing of divination sticks, or even the gathering of knowledge from knowing the people, the village, the town.

I looked at the goat that was not just a goat. I knew it was real.

Goat did not care. She was not in my mind and had her own story to tell me. Goat seemed to laugh, informing me that she'd have butted the woman on her backside and eaten all her crops. I did not laugh at this, no matter how much I wished to.

It did not remove my responsibilities. I had a duty to help the town.

I did take the time to show the town head not only the picture of the plant, and the slightly wilted specimen wrapped in waxed cloth, but also the goats, whose milk should not be gathered for drinking or cheese, but thrown out. At least for a few days. He promised to look for more of the plant and destroy it with my instructions or mark it so that people would not touch it. He overrode the farmer's objections and quarantined the goats till their milk had been gathered for a full week. His overabundance of precaution told me he did not care for the woman himself.

I didn't mind. He became effusive in his thanks and gifts to me, trying to ensure that Tages would not be angered for the farmer's rudeness to me, for she had followed not long after and was infuriated that I had the presumption to tell her how to treat her goats.

She was already breathing better, her heart was clearly giving her the proper amount of energy, and her rash was visibly better. I hoped my demands weren't fueled by my peevishness for having to prove myself. Yet the Twisted Flower had been clear, as had Goat.

I told him that I would be going home soon, and that we'd make more antidote for this plant fairly soon. I had used all of the healing herbs I had found, though I showed him what to look for. I gave him the rest of the salve I had been carrying for weeks because Tages had added it to my supplies.

Clearly, he had known I'd encounter a poison arrow plant of some sort. He was sure to know I'd use it and run out. "I'm sure he knows, however, to make more," I said.

With that last healing, I turned my feet back to Tages's house and the villages along the way. There was little for me to do but care for a spider bite—fortunately not too toxic—and celebrate a marriage. When I was on the main road to Thefartown, I heard a horse galloping through the woods, and stepped off the faint road. It was Larce on a white horse.

"You have been out healing, I see."

"Yes," I said. "And I have a staff."

He shook his head. "It has bells on it."

"Yes, so young hunters don't shoot me. Even if they use their arrows for taking down fowl, I'd rather not have to pull arrows out of me. Don't worry, I can still use it to defend myself. Or would you rather them shoot me?"

He laughed. "You are right. If they shot you, Ravantha would destroy their village. Bad for her reputation as a worthy leader."

"Clearly. What are you doing out and about without your companion? I thought you and Marce rarely left each other's side."

"I have great business to do in Thefartown, so I go willingly from the companionship of my friends."

"For your uncle Aranthur?" I asked. "Is he still after Thielle's necklace and thinks Thefare will finally give it to him?"

"He's always after that and other divine relics. But no. That's not my errand."

He was not forthcoming. "Ravantha or Rasce?" I asked.

"No, well, not exactly. For Ravantha."

I prodded again. "Oh, and what business is that?" It wasn't merely to engage in conversation with someone I might consider a friend. I'd been seeing too much disquiet in various villages not to try and inquire what the lords or ladies involved might inspire.

"To hear if it's true that someone has included you in negotiations for a marriage."

"Tages?" I asked, appalled. "He would not promise me to

another without warning me." In fact, he couldn't. When Grandmother Turani had arranged the apprenticeship, I'd heard the negotiations. Marriage could only be arranged after I'd become a master or been released from my adept work. Impossible, as well, after I became a Master Doctor-Diviner, because then I'd have the power to choose for my own self.

"No, Thefare. He's guessed Ravantha is your mother—you look like her and have been visiting her quite often. Presumably, you have his brother's eyes."

Fuluns! I thought with a grimace. A rapist who had defiled one of Larce's cousins, as well as Ravantha. A horrid person, to be sure.

"I visited only once, and still don't believe she's my mother, so why believe he's my father? Many people around here have similar eyes. Regardless, he can't negotiate for me, either. I'm lawfully Tages's adept."

"From what I hear, that is not stopping him. Ravantha wants you to stay with her while this is sorted out."

I shook my head. "I must go back to my master," I said.

"She would have you go to her now."

"That is impossible. I must deliver items to my master and discuss a great many things with him." I had a poison plant in my bag I was keeping alive—struggling without dirt or water—along with plenty of the antidote plant I'd found along the way to add to our supplies and other plants that could be turned into Medicine. My bags were heavy. If he wanted to help, he could have offered to let his horse carry what was clearly a well-filled bag on my back. I wouldn't turn back to the Westvell, regardless of anyone's wishes. I had plenty of information Tages needed to know about the health of the region he'd sent me to heal and observe. I had not only a duty to do as he asked, but also an obligation to a community. A potentially serious one.

"She won't accept that," he said.

"She doesn't have a choice. I have my own work, and if I did not respect it, then the village of Resala will come across a plant that could kill them, and Tages won't have the antidote already prepared for them." I overstated the plant's threat, though it was quite possible for some hapless individual to react more strongly than most.

Larce grumbled. "Well, maybe I'll come to teach you while I'm there, and to let Tages know the situation—if it is as bad as I believe it to be."

"How could it? Thefare has no claim on me," I said. I did not add that Ravantha had no claim on me, either, but I knew that he firmly believed she should.

"You may be surprised what wealth and consequence can do!"

"What do you mean?" I felt a sudden chill.

I found myself in the defensive stance Larce himself had taught me.

Wealth? Surely, we were not poor, but many of our donations went to buy paper for notes and study, as well as books about plants and bodies. My own collection had been growing not only from gifts from Professor Cuintus, but those I'd purchased through Aule. Consequence? He was implying that Tages had none. This was ridiculous.

Tages was well-known throughout much of the country, not just this region.

However, I suddenly realized that while Tages might have been sharing more information with Vesalus and others about his studies of the lymphatic system, and was growing in respect in the learned institutions of the Great Cities, he was only a Doctor-Diviner to the lords and ladies of this land. It was possible they were infected by the well-deserved derision many of our colleagues incurred.

"Sen, Tages may be a great man, but he is not a lord. He has no real power."

"I've seen him demand clearing up a sickened well," I said, "from Thefare himself."

"Foolish girl. You do not understand! Thefare would do well to listen to a man who has the health of the land in his keeping. He would have to fix it or render it unusable, as was his *natural duty*. He would not do it because *Tages* ordered him to. Ever. The words of even the greatest Doctor-Diviner have no weight except as a suggestion to even a scrabbly lord like Thefare."

I turned and walked down the road. I did not want to hear this. Thefare was not really such a scrabbly lord. He had something Ravantha's father had wanted. Not just him, but Marce's father as well—something they had prized enough to be a worthy exchange for all of the Westvell.

Larce did have a horse, and he could easily catch up with me.

"Sen, you must understand—these people value you."

I laughed. "Value me? Not *me*! I am just a *thing* to them. You made that quite plain."

I thought of that broken necklace in my bag. It was another object of value. A thing they would make use of. Whatever its real power, or whatever beauty it once had, was lost. Except, I'd seen Ravantha's rape in a vision when sleeping near the Tree, as if I were within the amber pendant of Thefare's half of the necklace.

And this before I even had the other part of it in my possession.

Broken, tarnished, defiled, there was already a complete *copy* of it in gold, shining and new, and worn by Thefare's wife not but a few weeks ago as the superior item. Its pendant dangling in her cleavage during a healing rite. It wasn't this new shining necklace that was valued. If what I had seen in the various villages I'd visited was real, there might very well be a war because of the broken one.

The part I had in my bag seemed to burn like a pocket sun, dripping golden light upon the road for Larce and me to see. Jackal emerged onto the road and danced in its light, smirking and laughing at me. His bark was high-pitched. Larce couldn't hear it, but his horse was flicking its ears in some consternation.

I continued. "All my life, they've ignored me, rightfully believed Ravantha's daughter must be dead. Now, because of a passing similarity in my face and eyes, they think I must be this long-lost daughter. It's ridiculous."

"And you don't think it possible?"

I had been Tages's student for too long. I believed him when he said there were no other women as far along in their pregnancy as Ravantha in even the farthest possible area for me to have been somehow exposed in the same region as her daughter. And yet Grandmother Turani's home was remote and lonely. Not even Tages could say for sure when I'd been found. And he visited most often during my childhood. No matter how often I listened for my ancestors—Tages and Velia would be so thrilled!—they remained silent.

I did not have other proof, however.

Even before I went on my rounds, I had gone back to Grandmother Turani's home and tried to find more evidence of my past that she might have kept. Surely, she'd have kept something. Still, like the last time, I had not found a baby's gown with beads and amber sewn into it. Ravantha had described the gown she'd made, and claimed it would be proof I was her daughter. And I had looked. I had nothing.

Having some freedom, I'd spent a couple of days there. The only revelation was a secret box of ancient love letters, or rather prayers, that fell apart in my hands. In different handwriting, the letters seemed to be to Turani, or even Thielle, to bless love and union. A strange thing, as if long-lost votives to the ancient temple her house once had been remained. Many people had called Grandmother Turani "Old Mother Love," playing on one of Thielle's names. Perhaps she'd preserved these things, as the house was an abandoned temple of that goddess.

But still no baby gown. It was possible that she'd sold the silver and beads for some reason, but she'd had other rich mementos in her money box from former visitors looking for herbs. I gathered some of it to fill my own pockets to use in getting more equipment and books for my own use. I'd doubted that she'd sell gems from a baby's gown when she hadn't sold any of those other things, much less the parts of the necklace she clearly had owned for some time.

I could not help it. I was still skeptical.

"Sen," Larce said, "do you not think there is some possibility?"

I looked up. His expression was petulant for having been ignored for some time.

"Okay, I will admit to you, however it irks me: It is possible. It is only *one* hypothesis among many others *that cannot be proved.*" I laid as much emphasis on my words and voice as I could. "There is no proof except their hope and a trick of timing. A dispassionate view removes the idea of any familiarity. I have similar skin tones as many people here—darker than your Aranthenvellian skin—and the long black hair is common enough, as is my eye shape. I do not want, or need, to borrow in their glory, however noble their status may be. I have status of my own, a profession I'm learning and proud of."

Larce shook his head. "You've been around Tages too long."

"Long enough!" I said.

He walked his horse alongside me for a while longer. I realized he did not wish to leave me. Either he felt he was my protector—even though I hadn't needed it for the whole month I'd been traveling alone—or he felt he could convince me of his sense of right. He spent time, after a brief but blessed silence, trying to press his knowledge and expectation of me, finally letting slip in his exasperation the name, "Sen Ravanthine," like an angry mother did when calling her child using their full name.

I was angered at his revealed lack of respect. "That's not my name!"

"That is what many now call you."

I stopped. He turned his horse. "Come on, Sen. Can't you see her parentage is a gift? Better than any patronage?"

I looked at him and realized he would not leave this alone, nor me, as long as our route followed the same road. I gritted my teeth and felt how close Jackal's Way always was. Especially with him laughing at me. Without leaving the road, I muttered in Ndeb, and the horse shivered and whinnied. Horseflies bit at its hindquarters, just where its tail couldn't reach. It took Larce some time before he could get her under control, and I was long out of sight before he could.

I chuckled to myself. "That was bad of me." I then felt guilty for tormenting the innocent horse with biting flies.

But Larce had not been contented by the conversation either, and made no attempt to waylay me again, even if he'd somehow found the opportunity to do so. I was now quite safe from his sight. He went off on his business—perhaps the only one of the three friends who could walk into Thefare's court without suspicion.

Chapter Five

The month of Tuvath, the height of summer

The midsummer month of growing, where fields grow rich and ripe, could be a season of no rain, though rare. Heat that baked the soil could destroy not just Rasce's or Ravantha's grain—wheat or oats—but also the wild grasses that fed cattle. The height of summer might bring not wealth, but suffering.

In our territory, Tuvath was better known only as the mother of Thielle and Nhor; up north, she was also the mother of Persipnei, who lives in the underworld with the God of the Dead. Whoever her daughters were, she was married to Hehunn, a god of hunting, while she was a Goddess of Summer Bounty. She was also significant as an aspect of time.

The true significance of Tuvath was already lost in the mishmash of myth and tales and stories that have become more popular. Growing up, I thought interesting to see how legends tied all four goddesses together—bound by time, as well as growing and dying of the seasons and nature. For some reason, I always envisioned Tuvath, in this season, as holding the hands of her younger daughters throughout the trials that they would face. However motherless I sometimes felt, I found the season heartening.

For the most part, the weather of this month is fine, as Tuvath is accepted as a fairly benign goddess. In grain lands, her symbols often showed growing grain. In Thefarland, she was shown off symbolically or illustrated with cows placidly eating in the fields, getting fat... for the slaughter, of course, in later months. The wild grasslands upon which the cattle fed also seemed to explode with beauty, sharing their bounteous wealth in the growing heat.

Tages was busy in his laboratory. As he approved of my work, he continued to send me further afield than ever before, still without exploring new ways to divine. Tages said nothing of what Larce had suggested, and even if he hadn't divined anything, surely Velia might tell him of that nasty, improbable rumor. Still, I was quite grateful to ignore it and steep myself in the work I loved.

I'd return with my journal filled with drawings, and my bag full of new plant samples, and empty of healing herbs and other potions I'd distributed and used on my journeys—no matter, as I could always find healing herbs to hand along my travels.

While we gathered or made supplies for more trips out, Tages and I would spend time together going over my notes. He, in turn, would tell me about his studies. On my second return, he gleefully told me more of his growing study of the lymphatic system and how it was helping his correspondent, Vesalus, learn more of how the body worked. Vesalus, being only an anatomist, and Tages, being one who had been studying the effects of infection all of his life.

They now had drawings and diagrams.

I exclaimed, "That's why sometimes the lower jaw becomes inflamed, or the armpit, when someone is sick! It is fending off the illness, swelling even as it fights, like a fever fueling its healing fight."

Tages smiled. "You are an apt pupil!"

We looked over the diagrams and discussed what new knowledge there was about this mysterious system in the body. He sent me off again, soon after, visiting villages to the east and south, which included seeing the coast on an errand for Tages. This time with a long list of things he could only get from the port city of Thiti, named after an ocean goddess. He wanted me to visit a couple of Doctor-Diviners along the way to assess them with my own eyes, as well as find a place to stay at need.

The endless vista of the ocean was daunting. As I turned from the coast to make my way to Doctor-Diviner Thucer's tiny cabin, I could hear the waves, similar to, but much louder than, the softer play of wind upon grain or grass, or dancing with swaying trees as they made music.

Meeting these Doctor-Diviners farther from Thefarland, I'd become even more aware of how much knowledge Tages passed on to me. In these travels, I attempted to respect their art; mostly, they just wanted news or gossip. They housed me only because I was Tages's adept. They did not acknowledge that I had anything to offer.

I had not thought to meet a supposed healer worse than Bathos.

Thucer didn't even bother to pretend. I watched as Thucer randomly dosed his patient, hoping for the best.

There were no symbols drawn; his supposed Medicine was

given in a fiction of nonsense sounds—Bathos at least had *some* Ndeb—and so he certainly did not call upon ancestors, much less inquire into the truth of what was unseen.

He was bewildered by his patient continuing to sicken. I had a good hypothesis from observations, though I could not do an examination.

"It is a form of grippe," I said. "You could try…"

Thucer refused to let me continue.

"You're only an adept. What do you know?"

"Tages is an excellent teacher!"

The man waved me off, and I shut my mouth. I was suddenly glad that his nonsense was limited to words and the waving of his hands. He certainly did not call upon his community to aid his patient or the man's family as minor doctors, or just to give succor. That was one thing I could be grateful for, as grippe could be contagious.

I had plenty of the healing herb to help, and knew where other palliatives could be found, even just along the roadway. The man refused to use my supply. When the patient came back the next morning, Thucer merely poured what could only be called folk remedies down the man's throat, clearly hoping one would work.

I'd tried to hand him some of my tinctures, but he didn't take them. "Go off, girl!" he said.

I sighed and stepped back and watched as he made a botch of things. I wanted, I'll admit, to scrape his Master scar off his right hand.

He didn't even have respect for the scientific process— which was threaded throughout even traditional Doctor-Diviner work, and not exclusive to modern science—to document what he'd tried, so he could use it later or not. I despaired for his patient and the community.

And then I remembered something from recent letters from both Aule and Professor Cuintus, who had introduced me to much of the lore of modern taxonomy, aiding my studies of botany.

I didn't know how bad a social gaffe I might be committing by just leaving, but I could not abide Thucer's company and the significant proof of why many were growing to see Doctor-Diviners as quacks. I went in to search for more intelligent company.

In the coastland, with the influence of the city of Thiti, as well as the education of the Great Cities, our art had started becoming superstition and not medicine. With reason!

Straight dosing of people, or surgery, was being called medicine, without seeing how so many other elements were woven together to cause illness. There were fewer ritual Medicines performed to sway angry ancestors, or give power to the herbs and medicine we gave our patients.

I noticed that people got their meat from butchers. I could guess, thinking of both Kutu and Jackal, that hunting was now a sport, not bred out of necessity to feed, or even to protect villages from predators. With less hunting, there were fewer stories and lore of any of the nature spirits. I hated the town for its almost spiritless landscape—no matter how vibrant it seemed otherwise, with people.

Seeing the city from the outskirts, I'll admit I was cowed. For the first time, I felt like a country bumpkin, and I felt every ounce of my inexperience.

In the streets of the port city, I did not see any of the

rough-hewn stone and brick buildings, or even echoes of them. Here were cleaner lines and statuary that displayed both old-fashioned, loose gowns, diadems, and veils, and modern ones. The streets were muddy to start, and the horses, chariots, and carriages made them worse than muddy. The buildings were tall, many of clean-cut stone, and made with old and new artistry that made Thefare and Ravantha's castle or manor pale in comparison with even some of the clearly less noble residences I could see. Merchants lived in well-built houses that Thefare would have envied for their style, if not size.

Aule had written about Gavius, noting him as something of a friend. He studied in Jambrone, mainly anatomy. Some of the focus of his own study was lessening the dangers of cutting into a person and minimizing pain, which is where he'd met Cuintus—herbs being a source of pain reduction and sedatives.

Currently, he was staying on the outskirts of Thiti, watching over a friend's healing practice, while they went to his wife's former home to celebrate a wedding and other events. I asked for directions and got lost and found my way again in mid-afternoon. Knocking at his door, a servant gave me entrance.

I was led into the room, and it was clear the man was surprised that a Doctor-Diviner's adept would bother to approach him. My clothing gave me away. Tebenna and robes and pack.

"What is it? Do you need my help?" he asked.

"Forgive me, but Professor Cuintus said you were here," I said, using that name, instead of Tages's son, Aule's, borrowing on that authority. "I wished to meet you. I am Sen of the Woods, adept to Tages of Thefarland."

"By the bright bells of Turan!" he cried out. "I had no idea!" His brown eyes sparkled with joy.

I blushed. "How could you? We rarely travel here. I came to the city to get items off a list Tages gave me, and—" He interrupted me.

"Sen! Yes, of course. I've been reading some of your work on healing plants. Aule said I might enjoy the discussion of your Ndeb language-embedded plant and healing classification, comparing it to the taxonomy Cuintus teaches." His eagerness was infectious. He stood up, then remembered himself. "Please sit!" He called to the servant for something to drink.

"I did not know they had finally printed the volume," I said. "I have not been home to see if Aule had written me."

"I believe this is mainly your work, but knowing the university, they would not have printed it without Aule or Professor Cuintus."

My smile was wry. "I know that Aule helped me put it in the style of the work and papers that the students and teachers write. His help was considerable. I'm honored that you are reading it."

Gavius smiled at me, and it lit his entire face. I felt a happy glow. He said, "I wanted to know what healing plants were nearby, so I could gather them and make medicines for my patients while I am here. I do not have access, any longer, to the well-built laboratories of the university, or access to their apothecaries."

I knew that he was referencing not the people who made potions or teas, but rather the place where these medicines were kept.

"The book should help," I said.

"I did not know you were a woman."

I shrugged.

"Is there a Doctor-Diviner I can have guide me to these

plants?" he asked eagerly.

I snorted. "I wouldn't trust Thucer as far as I could toss his threshing basket. Thucer is another reason I came."

I told him of Thucer's sick patient. "I do not know much of how a Doctor-Diviner works. I will say the illness has no ancestor causing grief due to neglect. I am speaking of observation and diagnosis, which your own studies surely encourage you to do. Pure and simple, from what little I could observe, I'd hypothesize it is a grippe. The family should have support, at least infusions to aid their immunity. Mountain Ganos—an herb—is useful for both."

"Grippe, of *any* sort, will spread," Gavius said.

I nodded. "Especially in Thucer's hands. He has not even a good foundation in the art of a Doctor-Diviner to heal the man, much less prevent the growing illness."

I set down my bag and brought out the plant I had gathered on the roadside.

"It was originally from the more mountainous regions to the north, and I believe originally came from the lands across the straits. But it grows weedlike and is also a pretty addition to an herb garden. It is tasteful in foods, but as an infusion, or better yet, an extract, it will improve the immune systems for those at risk and those who were ill."

"It is not a dangerous illness, is it?" he asked. "I mean, currently?"

"No, but the weak—children or the elderly—might sicken enough to die, if not treated properly. If you have pen and paper, I can draw you a more detailed illustration of the plant and what to look for in flower and in greening times."

He readily supplied me with both. He was grateful for the

drawing, and he and I talked long into the night about plants and healing herbs. I drew him other useful herbs I knew he could find in the area.

It was in this moment I realized how and why modern taxonomy might have value. It might strip a plant's usefulness away, but it allowed a person to find the plants based on detailed descriptions. Gavius, having studied some botany, could use this to find the plant in the wild.

The paper he had exclaimed about might be weaker because I hadn't quite understood this. I could hardly contain my excitement. I wanted to get back to my hut and begin the work in earnest.

The next morning, Gavius showed me the workroom. "This is all I have to work with, and no good apothecary—person or storefront. It is meager enough, as you can see. I miss the labs in Jambrone!" He might be studious, as his neck's curve and the stooped shoulders told me, but he was not one to stay in a lab or library. His body was strong. "Mine is probably insufficient," he said apologetically.

I laughed. "It's probably rudimentary compared to the equipment in the university, but far better than what I began to learn with. There is a lot you can do with what you have here. It will be rougher, and potentially your decoctions and extracts might not be as strong, but they will work."

"After years of the best equipment, there's a great deal to learn in how to make do with little!" he admitted.

"Perhaps you can go back to your university and teach a class on being a physician in the wilds."

Gavius laughed. "Perhaps, but I will be finishing my studies on surgery. That's more my passion. I am learning how limited my studies were in my months here, however. Help me?"

Gavius was familiar enough with the process that it took all of ten minutes to show him how Tages and I had worked for years. There was only a little more preparation of the ingredients we needed to get them where the equipment could handle them.

Afterward, rather like a treat, he talked about the new understanding of blood and the heart.

"Galen had it wrong," he said. "It is a circulatory system."

"Tages has been entertaining himself by how wrong he is, and learning what he can."

Gavius shook his head. "Galen is getting a poor reputation, but you must remember that he challenged thinking, which led to what we are learning now. Without him, we could never have known the brain was the seat of thinking. At one point—and maybe you haven't been able to study some of the more ancient teachings—people thought the brain was something that radiated out of the extra heat from the heart. He couldn't always work with humans, and made mistakes looking at cow brains and sheep brains. He knew that human brains were more complicated than animals' brains, and all the folds had to do something more."

"I have only seen animal brains, I'll admit."

"Oh? Have you?"

"Tages had us dissect quite a lot of various animals, even ones we were going to eat for dinner, so we'd know the body. We've dissected more than one animal. We have investigated the human body in what books Aule sends us from the university. No dissections of people, though. That is still forbidden by the culture of our province. Besides, the ancestors would pitch more than fits."

Gavius chuckled, and I realized he didn't believe me.

"Ancestors or no, those people who do dissect the bodies in the school of anatomy aren't generally well regarded by the living, either."

"I imagine not, but what did Galen learn, then?"

"That the brain is surrounded by the special senses, as if they are 'servants and guards of a Great King.' He was also fascinated by the spinal column."

"My main interest is plants, I'll admit, and what they can do for the body. Tages is fascinated by the lymphatic system, but tell me of this circulation!" I said, trying to get back to the point of the discussion. I'd heard and been part of too many discussions about Galen's ancient learning and teaching to think it could go anywhere.

"A man named Harcle showed it to me."

"Can you show me?"

"I can't show you on my arm. I'll want both hands."

"Then do it on me."

"Do not worry. I will not cut into your skin with needles or knives," he said, gathering up a ligature. I knew that, despite his education in anatomy and surgery, the hesitation to cut into the body remained strong. Then I realized that he might think that I, as a Doctor-Diviner adept, might hesitate, that my more supposedly superstitious attitudes might find any kind of bloodletting repugnant, or even immoral.

"I am not worried," I said. "I do not agree with practices like using leeches, for instance, a lesser bloodletting practice, because I do not think it helps the body as much as a good tincture that would boost the immune system. I do think once we know more that there are ways to heal the body. Removing tumors that destroy the body might save it better when herbs cannot, and do not. As we learn more, we can heal more! Talk to Thucer if you want foolishness."

He grinned at me. "I should have known, as you are Aule's friend, for you clearly have both a curious and scientific mind."

He tied the ligature around my upper arm.

"It helps if you make a fist," he said.

The veins in my arm popped up.

He put two fingers from either of his hands over one of the veins, and then rubbed one of the veins clear of blood down toward my hand. He carefully placed his finger on the other side, leaving a spot open about half an inch.

"Now watch. If Galen was correct, then the blood would fill up the empty spot."

He lifted the finger holding the upper spot. Nothing happened.

"Well, well, well. I'll have to show this to Tages when I get the chance, if he hasn't heard about it yet."

Gavius grinned at me. "I'm not done. And... for the proof."

He lifted the spot closer to my hand, and the empty spot filled. Obviously, the blood was going *toward* the heart, and destroying Gavius's ancient assertions. I laughed in appreciation.

Gavius laughed with me. "A harmless experiment." He looked at me. His expression was wry, but his eyes seemed to brighten. "Even with that interesting book you wrote, I did not know a Doctor-Diviner adept could appreciate something like this as well as I would."

His smile was warm. We talked more about circulation, and the studies he wished to pursue when he got back to the university. We talked more about the practical use of plants he would soon need if my observations and hypothesis were correct. I felt my heart warm to this man, handsome enough to catch any woman's eye, but it was his mind that appealed to me. I had a feeling I could talk with him for hours.

For the first time, I wished I could go to the university and study.

Together we went to the markets. Gavius guided me and negotiated better terms for the items Tages had requested. There were piles of the spice I knew as Ilatchi, and other aromatics like cinnamon, cardamom, and a pile of oranges.

Using money I might have spared for books, I bought some oranges for Gavius and me to share. They were still as juicy as I remembered, even while Gavius said they were rather early. There were piles of seafood I'd never known or heard of. However, Gavius hadn't known about local fare. There were piles of various cheeses I had not yet tasted. I showed him nourishing local plants in an off-market that was less popular because it was not as exotic, not having things that could come off ships from foreign lands. I explained the nutrients and tastes of various legumes and beans, and how well they went with various meats.

"I am surprised. I had not guessed that Doctor-Diviners have this wealth of knowledge. From what I had heard and read, I had not even guessed that the renowned Tages or Sen might be scholars. Forgive me."

"We *are* scholars, just not affiliated with a university proper except through friends. I've come to know some of our supposed colleagues; I can admit that you are not wrong to think that they know little. Many of them do not even know the language that is the backbone of our art. I suspect Tages, Cai, Aule, and I are the last who truly understand the language, along with Zelia to the north."

"And you are working on a book that tells of this lore?"

I smiled. "Yes, a book that describes the plants with modern taxonomy, which will help you, I have no doubt, but also explains their classification within the language of Ndeb—which is useful because it often describes *why* the plants are healing for different ailments of the body. Professor Cuintus is helping ensure that it is clear and that I have the taxonomy correct."

"I assure you that in rural areas it will be most useful!"

"Thank you."

He had me explain to him more of the lore of ancestors and nature—for he had met, a time or two, those who had distrusted his lack of spiritual insight. I knew that he would be a good physician, for he became emotional as we discussed the value of community in Medicine. He took notes about many things, and as a gift of thanks for my help, I gained another book on various insect bites and how they could poison a person. We also talked a great deal about surgery. Having done minor surgery in the past, it was marvelous to have this information on the deeper elements.

"If we could cut into a person and remove tumors, would that not be a good thing?" he said.

"But wouldn't you be in danger of cutting into any veins or arteries?" I asked.

"That is why we have a school of anatomy now, in an old, unused temple. You would have to truly understand the body."

I nodded. "That is the important thing. But what of the illness that could come in through those open wounds?"

"Everything, I think, would need to be clean. But we only work with cadavers, when we can get them. So far, it is still illegal or immoral to cut into a healthy person," he said. "Which is why students who learn there are often looked at with a very leery eye."

"You are frightening, cutting into flesh."

"We are like the old Goddess Nhor, I think—some versions of her, where we are more frightening than the illness we might one day cure."

I laughed. "But you are not yet seen with such holy grace."

"No, we're often seen as little better than butchers, or surgeons who cut off a badly wounded leg or arm."

The discussion of theory went far into the night.

I felt deep regret that I had to leave the next morning. The exchange of information was unlike any I'd ever had before. He loaded me down with herbs and spices that I could not find on my own—and Thucer hadn't bothered to share, if he even had any. He also gave me a precious tin of Yezginy tea. Gavius walked with me on my way out of town, so I could point out plants he could gather alongside the road. He left me in the afternoon after a roadside luncheon to return home, his mind and bag full.

I returned home, thinking that with a modern physician, I had better hospitality than I had with one of my supposed colleagues. There was joy in being respected as a scholar, as a colleague. It gave me hope for my future. I was warmed by more than just the sun. I thought about his smiling face. I beamed because I had realized how much I'd liked him.

Chapter Six

A copy of Aule's and my book was waiting for me.

Tages didn't give me time to put things away in my hut. We dove into work, poring over my journals of plant life— so many that I'd kept my diary separate, filling volumes with sketches and filling my shoulder bag with specimens. I felt renewed confidence in our Medicine—it went beyond the mumbo-jumbo Bathos or Thucer spouted.

I noted, after hours spent with my mentor, that Velia was not present. Observing the evidence of a long absence, it seemed far longer than I'd ever known. The place was remarkably disordered.

Tages's worktable in the house never spilled beyond those confines, even without counting the laboratory in my hut.

I missed her suddenly. Competent, curious, and quite consequential to the household. Each time I returned, the house would be neat, and the only off note was how often she'd pester Tages. Ever since the months of spring, she was still trying to drag

Tages away from this dusty desk, dotted with open books, journals, papers, rotting fruit, and molding bread. A mess that had expanded much further into their living space than I could ever have imagined.

"Is it twins? Or a breech birth?" I asked, thinking about times when I'd been his apprentice when a slighter disorder had happened. "Is that why Velia is away?"

He dismissed it with a shake of his head, "No, no, nothing like that," and continued to look for some reference with one of my journals in his other hand.

Despite her competence as a housekeeper, I missed even her continued complaints that were like scratches on a wall. I usually escaped to work in my hut, but suddenly, it was a sound I wanted to hear.

She'd given up the idea that they'd have a windfall from Lord Aranthur—far richer than Thefare, Rasce, or his daughter, Ravantha—for a healing that Tages, and his northern counterpart, Zelia, had apparently refused to give. Not because they did not wish to, but because it wasn't some angry ancestor causing an illness. It was something inherited from them, for his son, Marce, showed signs of having it, too. The current bass notes of her complaints were a lack of apprentices to help with the work. She suggested moving to Jambrone, to be closer to her beloved son, Aule, to leverage his connections—proved by so many letters now strewn about the room—to gain some kind of teaching appointment in the university.

Noticing the dust on his shoulders, the grease of his hair, I also saw how thin he'd become. He must have forgotten to eat.

Beside the fire, I noticed a large pot of stew. It was still warm because of the coals, but cooling. It had dried, apparently, as the fire went down. I rebuilt the fire, with Tages absorbed again with my journals, and added water to the stew. The beans had been cooked so long it almost had the consistency of porridge, even the large chunks of carrots were soft. I guessed that the only reason the bits of meat weren't leather was because of whatever broth had been in it to begin with.

It was still flavorful, as anything Velia might make, but it clearly had simmered too long, and some of the herbs had given it sharp notes.

At least it's not burnt, I thought. And that because Tages probably forgot to tend the cook fire.

I handed him a bowl and forced his attention to it.

"Where's Velia?" I asked again.

"Away," he said, and dismissed the topic.

"Tell me more of your travels," he said. "I'm assuming that you preceded another one of your letters."

I noticed that he had a stack of them, though they were mostly notes written upon my return, of what I observed from the various villages I visited, making clear the tensions along the Thefarland and Westvellian border. They peeked out from a stack of books.

Pulling them free, I put them on top of the book he'd been reading. I then described to him the troubling situation I'd witnessed at the coast. I told him that I'd discussed it with Gavius, giving him the herbs to do the healing that would no doubt be needed.

"That was good of you. Healing ought not be divided, as we have seen, or we would not be drafting articles or getting books published with those scholars from the city."

"I was worried you might agree with what Thucer might

easily see as a betrayal."

"You should not have worried. He is the one betraying our art. Gavius is not. And if you had not done what you did, then many people might sicken without palliatives or remedy. I see, however, you have more on your mind than this."

"Doctor-Diviner Thucer muttered nonsense, and never divined the cause of the patient's illness. It made me wonder something. There have been times we've seen the ancestors of a patient or family, angered by neglect. The family and community come together and show their care. We've seen a plant spirit attack, as well as a patient's own guilt attack."

"Yes," said Tages. "What is it you ask?"

"There are other things unseen in our work, aren't there?"

"How do you mean? I think you are not speaking of what I might divine were my inner eyes clearer, or of those things only you can see, like the Tree at the ruins of Jammon's temple."

"Yes," I said. "Like various grippes, or winter respiratory illness and fevers. Or other ailments that are clearly not related to an ancestor or plant. Or like the kolephera outbreak that is carried by water."

"Ah. Yes. I think I see what you are asking. You want to know if there are other unseen things a diviner might not see?"

"Yes."

He nodded. "Yes, you are a clever student! I believe there are. Sicknesses that pass by unseen means. Do people *touch* the taint that made someone ill, or does it travel by air? There was a plague, once, along the coast of the southern continent—a swampy and rat-infested region—that few knew how to combat. Many, many people died. That was a hundred years ago. What spreads that sickness? Was it a surprisingly potent curse, or something else? The rats or the fumes of boggy air?"

"Yes! If there are illnesses that are carried by water, unseen except in proof of filth or feces in the water, what kind of illnesses would be carried by air?" I asked. "And is it air? Or something else?"

"There are certain hopes I have from the university. Imagine machines to see more, explore more! Science may one day *prove* there are ways illnesses travel that are unseen!"

My shoulders expanded as I took a deep breath of shared excitement. Velia might be right: a university might very well be the right place for a Doctor-Diviner of Tages's caliber, or a scholar of such curiosity. But as I breathed a few more breaths, I considered something else.

During my adept initiation test, I'd seen both Tages's and Velia's ancestors clearly. I failed because I could not see my own. I could see a Tree that Tages could not see, though he could feel the blossoms I'd brought him and pieces of bark. I could walk with Jackal on his Way, and so could not only see Him and Crow, but venture into this spiritual pathway with growing familiarity.

Some sort of seeing device might not make all these unseen parts of our world visible. I reached out to Tages, lightly touching his sleeve, and noticed my hand trembled as I formed a question.

"As much as I respect Gavius, I cannot help but know that he misses the side of our art that deals with not only ancestors, but community, as well as at times, nature. That said, he enjoyed foraging with me and my books. Still, what if scientists lose the subtle parts of a Doctor-Diviner's art? The part that sees the spirit of a person, a malady, a truth, or a lie. That this unseen taint comes to those weakened by their own spirit, or that of an ancestor.”

"I do not know. Would you prefer we not explore?”

"No!” I shouted without hesitation. "We must! But already I see Doctor-Diviners reducing Medicine to potions and a lack of care, as both Bathos and Thucer prove. A physician does it better. I'm so afraid.”

"As am I.” He paused. "Remember that it is also possible that there are terrible physicians out there as weak as our colleagues. Come, I have something to show you,” he said, turning to his work desk, with books he was writing strewn across it. He pulled out a volume. "Look.”

It was a book written in Ndeb. My heart felt as if it would burst. "Oh, Master!” All that Turani had taught him filled those pages. The language we kept alive. The natural base of our art.

"That one is yours. I have another. Did you know that there are other root languages?”

"I did not know that,” I admitted.

He chuckled. "Another great benefit of Aule sending me random books that he hopes will interest me.” He pulled out a little volume. "Somewhere on the continent, far to the west, is a culture influenced by the ancient country of Tashihyel and the language *Geberesh*. Much of it is lost. I read here that once they spoke of a seen and unseen world, and that true practitioners of their priesthood could see both.” He opened the volume to show me. "Here is their word for the world, *ihyel*. See how they write?”

"Their letters are strange,” I said.

"They have transliterations throughout in the discussion. The word for the natural world is *ihyel*, but their word for the unseen world is *vhagas*. Their priests called *Bogeh* could see what they considered the true world, what they called *ihyelvhagas*. Isn't that wonderful?" he said, looking at the slim volume and turning pages.

"Yes," I said, thinking of Jackal's Way, and shivered.

Tages looked up at me. "In some ways, it was what we do when we work a Medicine."

I smiled and then laughed. "We investigate it in so many ways. Seen and unseen. It reminds me of Grandmother Turani talking of what she called the Three Rivers. Do you know them?"

"Not well. It is like the three colors of our Medicine. White, red, black. I could gather that they echo those rivers. Red being the natural world, black being the underworld, and white the world of Spirit and maybe the Divine. How we work, they are always intertwined."

I thought of Jackal's Way, and how, while the power of it seemed to flow like the water of a river, and it might even be considered another world, it felt more like it was a different view of the world, a different perspective.

I shook my head; it was still too much to easily comprehend.

Tages continued, without having seen my fit of nerves. "What we see as magic may one day be science."

I sighed. "Where is Velia?" I finally asked again.

"As I said, she is much with Ati and Arntlei, negotiating, planning."

I shook my head slightly. He had not said that.

"Negotiating what? Planning what?"

"I do not know. Women's work, as far as I can understand. She wanted me to send you over when you were free."

"We have half a book to still go through and samples to ensure will thrive."

"You are good at the reviving part. I'll let you do that, and bring the book along to discuss."

I was good at making plants I'd gathered come back to life. I'd marked them with symbols from the Ndeb language and prayed over them each night and morning on my travels, speaking the words evoked by the symbols taught to me by Grandmother Turani, as well as all I'd gained by Tages. Each morning and evening on the road, I'd tend all my plants, ensuring each plant was not too crushed. Now home, I planted them in pots and attempted to re-create their original environment as best I could. Anything poisonous was put in a special garden; ones we wanted to investigate more were carefully labeled as well with the number and page of the journals.

Tages sat nearby in the shade of a tree and read over a journal, discussing it with me as I worked getting plants safely into the ground.

I was covered in soil, sweating in the sun while Tages talked with me, when Velia came home. She was resplendent in fashionable clothes. I had never seen her in anything modern. Her bodice was rich with embroidery, her veil worn not over her face, but over her head, falling to either side, emphasizing and framing her lifted breasts.

"You're here?" she asked. "Why did you not inform me?"

I looked at Tages, who seemed just as surprised by her outburst, but said nothing. That familiar crease in his brow deepened. He glowered at her attire. As much as he loved modern science, he deplored modern fashion. He thought it unseemly. His own eyes drifted to her cleavage, and away in a blush.

I turned to her. "I did not know you needed me," I said.

"Yes, and *now*."

Tages stood up. "Forgive me, wife. I needed to discuss our work before I sent her to you. Her primary duty *is* to me and our work."

Velia shook her head. She came up to me. "Are you darker from sun or is that dirt? You're dark and dirty as a laborer! Tages, she's covered in filth, and I need her cleaned up for some women's work. She should have been ready hours ago!"

The words to ever make a man release even his own student. I looked at Tages for some information, bewildered. Hours ago? My return wasn't scheduled to the hour, but within a window of days.

"Let me go to my hut and get cleaned up," I said. "I needed to get the plants planted as soon as I could. I haven't even put my things away, but came to give Tages my notes and..." I did not say we got distracted. She was angry enough as it was.

"No. No time," said Velia. "We'll clean you up at the castle."

Tages let me go—taking my books, excepting my diary of my travels. I left him absorbed in my latest plant book, comparing the drawings to the beleaguered, but still surviving, plants from my travels. It was not unusual for Velia to commandeer me for some task; she'd done it for months when I was an apprentice, but not often in such an imperious way. She was clearly agitated, but I followed her dutifully, like I always had.

Chapter Seven

I was familiar with the masks of Medicine, or ceremonial paint, if the masks couldn't fit into our packs because of the amount of other symbolic items or herbs, tinctures, salves, or whatever else we might require were there.

The painted and fashionable glamour of celebratory women was not something I'd been raised with. The closest I'd come was during Hastia's Milk Tree ceremony. I had stayed with her mother, Arntlei, where grief and sorrow were our side of that three-day-long ritual. My role had been to keep her from running out into the night to find her dead or dying daughter. If there had been paint on Hastia's side, I hadn't seen it. When she'd come bursting into the house, not some girl, and not even a daughter, but a woman, Arntlei's equal, there was no paint upon her face.

Apparently, women had taken over some chambers in Thefare's castle again, in a fog of perfume, a cacophony of sound, and a confusion of color in fabric and paint.

My familiarity with fashion came through either Velia, or

even Ravantha, and was still unlike the riot of color on the diaphanous fabrics the women of Arntlei's compound wrapped me in—as well as gems, beaten coins, and the surprising instruments of curling hair or painting faces.

Hastia greeted me joyfully. "I'm so glad you are here! I won't feel so alone now!"

I was bemused by this, as we were surrounded by what must have been many of the compound's women, as well as palace women. The noise in the large chamber was astounding. Velia was clearly helping organize everything, though it was clear that most of the women knew how to dress and paint themselves.

Two older, sturdy servant women stripped me from my travel-worn adept gowns and scrubbed me till I was pink. Velia was scornful that not all the brown on my skin was dirt. My scalp was sore from how they now pulled it as they combed out snarls from their vigorous washing.

They draped me in an undershift so fine that I could see my body through it in the light. This was disconcerting, but I was marginally happier when they layered me with more of this fine stuff. They stood me up, and two women stood on stools working on my hair, braiding it with wires to hold it up. Hastia came and commented on the paints for my face, reminding them that the pattern must echo hers.

I noticed that many of the girls, including Hastia, all had that traditional paint on their faces, though many also wore the bodices of modern dress. I knew that they had painted my face white over my deep tan to where I matched all their white faces. I thought this odd, as Ati and Arntlei were rarely out of doors, and were already rather pale.

I was sure there were implications of divine blessing in the white, but there was no divine clay. To my eyes, all the women looked interesting. The white paint made for a stark contrast against their black hair and red accents of lips and decorations. I knew that as dark as I'd become after all my travels, the contrast must have been quite odd on me. Velia had once commented on paleness being status. If you were rich, you didn't get dark like a laborer. You could stay cool indoors. I wondered what they'd think of some of the sickly pale people I'd seen on the coast. Suddenly, I yearned for a glimpse of golden or bronze skin. My darker, tanned tones must have given these women fits.

Even after plucking my eyebrows, they sharpened the line of my already-dark eyebrows and lined my eyes with black. I knew that my lips must be red, as were the three circles on my brow, dotted with smaller circles in a sunburst pattern, but it was clear that after they'd painted my lips the same vibrant red, they'd not drawn the delicate circle on my chin the way they had with Hastia. I had two lines drawn down my chin.

The woman in front of me, a servant, also had lines on her chin, as did several others. She was dressed more finely than I'd ever seen her. I did not know her well, but I'd seen her before. She wouldn't let me speak to even ask her name. She stepped back, looking at me and touching me up, before nodding to whoever was behind me.

I felt something wrapped around my torso, but was unable to look as one of the women pulled something in my hair. Then I felt the bodice tighten, and another woman actually reached into the device and lifted my breasts, before tightening it again.

I was as near to real violence as I had ever come—quite ready to elbow the woman who had her hands on my breasts the way Larce had taught me and punch her in the face. But these women were defenseless, making me into a copy of them, and Hastia's exclamation, "Oh, that's so beautiful!" stopped me.

It did not occur to me till later that the horde of women had already overpowered me, and fighting back would have been quite the losing battle—and more, would have completely bewildered them.

Every single one of them seemed excited by whatever this function was that caused all this preparation and fuss. This was all for Hastia, it was clear, so undoubtedly it was meant for some part of her upcoming nuptials.

I scratched at my adept scar. I thought of how Gavius had looked at me in the market, and how there was a part of me that had liked that.

Would I feel differently about all this costuming and makeup were the celebration for me? Possibly. But he was a city-bred man, and I suspected that he'd be stunned by all the traditional paint, even if the bodice was familiar.

I could only sigh, realizing that I'd never allowed myself to even consider any kind of attachment along those lines. The only men I knew were Aule, who I knew couldn't even begin to be thought of in that way, or Cai, who had also been out of bounds, even had I considered even one of his advances to be welcome. I yearned, however, for the conversation with Gavius, or even Aule, and how bright their minds were. Either man could—and both had—viewed me with pleasure, but also as equals.

I felt as anonymous as any of the other women, which was a comfort to some degree. Why I was even there, when Hastia was clearly surrounded by women, seemed quite strange.

The powders and paint felt odd, and my hair felt heavy with all the coils and gems embedded in them. I tried to make a tea for my headache—from all the hair pulling as they coiffed me—but Velia and the others would not give me a moment to do anything but be dressed.

Whatever paint I'd used before for some Doctor-Diviner ritual, women's rituals were, apparently, far more elaborate and vibrant.

I'd had plenty of opportunity to watch Velia throughout all this—at least, when I could turn my head, or if she came into my view. She absolutely glowed so much with happiness that her eyes sparkled like Ati's jewels. It occurred to me that once she'd been not only part of celebrations like this, but had organized them. She clearly missed this from a lack of having daughters.

As if I were a puppet, I was swathed in fabrics and unfamiliar dresses, with my hair curled in ringlets. Velia made much of me and declared herself proud. I was painted with colors, but apparently without the gleaming brightness and finery that adorned my supposed half sister, which was fine by me.

Hastia was wreathed in perfumes, cloth, and paint. She loved every minute of it.

A diadem from her aunt's trove of jewels from the treasure room adorned her regulated curls, and family jewels adorned her wrists and neck. I wondered how Thefare had managed to wrest the gem from Ati's grip.

My questions as to why I ought to be there were not answered, except that at one point, Hastia held my hand in a sudden need of comfort, and then later came to me and said, "As you do not know the dance, perhaps it is best you stand with Casiea? She's doing her work well, but this seems far beyond her somehow."

I finally noticed the poor girl, watching all the young

women get ready. She was dressed very finely, but was the only other person in the room who wasn't thrilled by everything.

Poor little thing! I thought, noting that she looked even younger than her eight years. The paint on her face didn't quite make her as anonymous as any of the other girls and dancers. They made her look small. Her eyes were huge and bewildered. Even across the room, I could see that tears were marring the white on her cheeks.

"Look, she needs you. She's crying, and I can't understand why. Isn't all this so much fun?" Hastia asked.

"Hastia, she's lived in poverty all her life. What's happening is confusing."

"Is it?"

"Yes! Even I have no idea what's going on."

Hastia laughed. "And yet you are so well educated!"

"But I only have to deal with the rules and structures of your world when I have to do a ritual dance of healing, or help Tages do a ritual of divining. I studied hard for those dances. It's difficult to dance some of those steps in a heavy mask. It takes practice to make it not go askew, twist to look past my ear, and leave me blind." I laughed a bit self-consciously. "All this? I wouldn't know how to begin!" I waved my hands to encompass all the girls, the noise, the fabric, and jewels. "It's overwhelming."

She laid a hand on my arm. "Don't worry. It will be okay. I'm glad you're here!"

She led me to the poor servant girl, and I took her hand. Casiea could not recognize me.

"Casiea, it's me, Sen. Will you hold my hand so I can remember myself? I'm feeling a bit overwhelmed by all this."

She could only nod and grasped my hand in a grip so tight

I could not let go and escape into the night. A woman came and fixed her paint. I could see that speaking would overwhelm her and bring her to the tears she no doubt had been told to keep in or ruin her paint again. Her lip quivered, and she bit it, smearing her teeth with red. She also had a stripe on her chin, like I knew I did.

They tied more layers of gauze over my skirts, of a different color, and veiled the giddy weight of my hair.

As the girls got ready to process to the main hall, I realized that Casiea, Hastia, and I all wore similar colors. We were the only ones with a deep red underdress and a lighter red over the white. Our hair was also woven with wires, and the braids that were turned into loops all around our heads were the same. I wondered at this.

Velia was nearby, standing next to her two friends. Thefare's wife's corset seemed tighter than the last time I'd seen her, lifting her breasts that seemed to now serve as a display for the gold necklace and a complete copy of Thielle's damaged one in Thefare's vaults. Thielle might be a goddess of love and harmony. Her temple in Jambrone might now be a den of prostitution. It was the latter version of the deity, I felt, who would approve of the display of bauble and breast.

Velia noticed me and started to step toward me as they moved us toward the main hall. She touched Arntlei's arm. "What is this? Ati? Why is Sen in—" she began, but couldn't finish the question. The tide of eager dancers forced the three women aside.

I could only pass by and offer my expression of my own bewildered confusion.

I understood more of what was happening when we arrived at the great hall. The man with whom Thefare was negotiating with for Hastia's marriage was here. And to show off a wealth he did not have, Ati, Arntlei, and Velia—for some reason—had conspired to dress up as many young women as possible to show Hastia off, as if she had a greater entourage than she did in truth. All she had was little Casiea, and whatever wealth her uncle was willing to give, if his brother did not help with the bargaining.

"Lord Pesne," Thefare intoned, "greet your future bride, Hastia Fuluni!"

I raised an eyebrow at this. She was her own woman, and her name should be called out as Hastia Arntleni. The man greeted her, looking her over the way Ravantha had once looked me over, or Velia looked over her cows. He seemed to approve, with a shrug, but nodded.

"Come," Thefare said, "sit, eat, and she and her women will dance and serve you!"

While I had plenty of experience dancing, I would not have had time to learn what all these girls did to show off Hastia's ability to dance.

It was a shrewd move on someone's part. I saw Velia's calculating assessment of the girl in this. I knew Hastia was kind, but here was a grace few could compare with.

Her slight, gangly body during dance erased any lingering regret on Pesne's face. Dancing, Hastia was agile as a doe.

From my vantage, her dance made her beautiful. I could see also how the makeup brought out the better features of her face, only adding to the glory of her grace. More, I could see the sleek sensuality to her that was not seductive, but natural as her movements.

The dance was a celebration, and as I watched her, my heart swelled with joy for her.

Looking at her intended, I could see that even he admired

it, but he was clearly contemplating how he would possess such grace. He was a modern man, but he sported the signs of whatever deep traditions his country had. I suspected something along the lines of a Hunting Cult. His face had dramatic scars along his cheekbones. The baubles and gold that decorated his formal, modern jacket looked as if they had been broken apart from some traditional, clunky style of jewelry I'd not seen before. But it worked, and made a deep mockery of Thefare's attempt to blend tradition and fashion together, even with eyes and brows emphasized with paint.

I found myself beginning to hate how scruffy and uncultured my home country seemed. I thought about Gavius, and how I'd not felt that way talking with him, especially with how even more markedly a contrast there was between that city and even this once-modern castle.

I held Casiea's hand and watched. At various breaks in the dancing, signaled by Velia, Casiea took a bowl with savory roasted meats on skewers or fruits from the serving tables. She handed it to Hastia. The two went to the dais where the men sat. Casiea took the empty bowl, while Hastia offered the fresh to her intended. When he approved of the offering, she set it on the table next to him.

Even at this distance, I could see how Hastia's picture of him was of quite the romantic hero. Her eyes were visibly dilated, and her breathing deepened. Her dance became even more sensual, which he watched with considerable pleasure.

I just stood against the wall as a place for Casiea to aim in returning to her post. Each time I took her hand again, she was shaking and sweating. I could see the lines of sweat mar her makeup. I did what I could to comfort her.

I noticed Thefare leaning over and telling Pesne something as they were gazing toward little Casiea's retreat. The man looked us over for a while with a contemplative grin, and then back at his bride-to-be. Disconcerted, I turned my attention not to the girls now dispersing to speak to guests—those who were old enough to be married, some already married. As soon as the largest performance dance was over, the youngest ones disappeared through the doors where Ati stood. She shooed them back to an old servant woman, who guided them into the depths of the castle.

Ati turned back to enjoying the look of the light on the jewels she wore.

I turned my attention to the guests. There was little else for me to do but stand there, hold Casiea's hand, and try to make it through the feast.

Lines for more coupled dances began, with Hastia being led to the top of the dance by her intended, who looked down her cleavage, spare as it was.

The intense faces of most of the dancers told me quite a lot. These dances were not traditional, nor well-known. Clearly, the local men and women had been drilled into learning these patterns. I could see Velia's eye upon them all, and even the girls looked to her for approval when the dance finished, which she gave with a brief nod.

I noticed that many of the girls dancing had sweat beading along the edges of their paint, or under their arms, between their shoulder blades. I didn't know how they could stand it. I was sweating just standing there, wondering how much damp would make these layers of gauze less opaque. I shuddered.

Each time Velia looked at me, her own paint displayed a crease between her brows, nearly as thick as the lines on some of the women's chins. I wondered how much I was sweating in all this pomp.

One or two men thought to ask me to dance, but noted—I thought—the line on my chin and hesitated.

For a trained observer, it took me too long to notice that no girl dancing had that line. I also realized, with burning fury, that only servants—well enough off in their own right, though some were—wore that line.

Tages's adept had been painted like a mere servant. What was Velia thinking? But I realized that she hadn't seen it painted on my face. It was probably the line on my chin, and the colors they'd added that had struck her as we moved out into the hall. She'd not make a fuss in such a public arena.

Tages's adept, her husband's adept, reduced to servitude. That diminished her value as well, line or no line on her chin. I knew her temper. Whatever she felt for me, what rage must she be keeping calm under all her paint, skirts, and cinched up as tight as her corset?

It was clear to me how much they'd done with curling my hair and paint then. They had obscured me completely with paint and baubles, even while I stood in plain view, the tops of my breasts lifted to the air for Pesne and all the men to view. A girl discarded a veil nearby, removing one seemly layer from the heat. I took it without compunction and covered myself up as best I could.

For most of the night, Larce was there, sometimes nearby, and he did not notice me. At one point, his eyes passed over me, but without any recognition whatsoever. I could not tell if this was because he was ensuring that he was otherwise unknown by anyone in the area, especially as any connection to me might lead back to Ravantha.

He was related to Aranthur, a man still vying for the original necklace so well displayed in wholeness and gold, lifted by Ati's cleavage. So, deception about any association seemed remarkably thin.

I wondered if Larce had already evaluated the value of this copy, versus the tarnished one in the vault that supposedly could heal, but never had. Still, it was strange that he was here, and had been, apparently for some time. Surely he would have known by now if the rumor that had supposedly brought him here was valid.

His eyes kept scanning the crowd as if looking for someone. He looked at me a number of times and simply did not recognize me. My face was as distorted and as different as when I wore a healing mask.

I did not eat much, and drank even less, and watched as more than one man and woman drank of the potent local wine, with quite clear effect. While Velia disliked the growing tone of a bawdy house, neither Thefare nor Pesne seemed to mind. They were enjoying the view damp gauze gave them—however much still, thankfully, obscured.

Long after I was ready, the girls were sent off to a large room where we could sleep, rescuing Hastia from the growing certainty of impertinent looks and touches from the man she would one day bed in wedlock.

I thought it odd that only a few girls dispersed to their homes, and that Hastia and I were sent to this room together, as Arntlei's house in the compound was not far off. It was a different room from the one where we'd all gotten into costume. Pallets were laid out. I sighed, disoriented and unable to find my way back to that room. I wanted my bag, as it had a number of potions in it—always—and my head was pounding with the unaccustomed noise and heat. I wanted to drink a gallon of water with a tincture that would ease my pain. I wanted to go home, but was trapped in so much now damp finery.

Chapter Eight

Casiea was long gone, finally able to join the other little girls, to parts unknown. I watched the girls help each other out of their bodices, and finally, they helped me. I had been struggling to get my hair un-baubled. My head throbbed, but they were all still trembling and chittering with excitement. They were able to get out most of the jewels and wire, and we stripped down to the last layer of shift. It was hot in the room, so I was grateful that while I felt nearly naked, my skin could finally breathe.

Velia came in and brought us all something to drink as we prepared for sleep. I took a few sips from my cup, but did not like it. I heard a jackal howl, despite the noise in the room, far off in the hills. I shook and nearly dropped the cup. Velia steadied the cup in my hands.

"Don't spill," she said, with a smile.

"Thank you," I said, feeling formal.

"You need to drink more," she said. "It's been a long day,

and it will help you rest. You must be as overexcited as all the other girls here. What noise they're making!"

"What is it?"

"Just some herbs I told Ati's maid servant how to brew, as I was busy. I told her what to use from their medicinal stores."

I did not need the jackal's howl to pause. She couldn't see that I was not as excited as these other girls, still chattering and tittering about whatever they'd experienced. Something in me rebelled. I took the cup, smiled, and pretended to drink more. She seemed content with that, and did not check the level of the potion in the mug, offering it to the next girl with a smile.

It was not till I dozed beside some of the other girls, grateful that the noise of their enthusiasm had finally died down, that I had an inkling of what was in that tea. A root herb that causes sleep. Amantile, it was called. Good for chronic insomnia, but too strong for aiding any normal sleep.

Thinking of Jackal's warning, I tried something new. I needed help. I'd met one plant spirit—could I call on another?

It took ages, but in my stupor, my mental words slurring, I called upon the plant's spirit. It was present, having had part of its root cut to make this tea. As soon as I could see it, I reached out to it and, in my dreaming state, fought to hold it.

"You are being misused!" I said to it, grabbing onto it so hard, I almost left my body.

It, he—the spirit more potent than the root of the plant— denied this. Or rather, more specifically, denied he was being used for any ill cause.

I ripped Amantile out of his spirit soil. "This is what they're doing! Help!"

I fought with him, using every effort my sleepy body had. I

showed him that we were being *forced* to sleep—not that we needed it. With my mental words slurring still, I explained I'd only had two sips, but I was overcome. The plant saw his power, gloried in it for a while, but it was a slow, sleepy plant, and took time to realize that he did not want to cause death to some poor girl.

I told him some of the girls were smaller than me, less powerful than me, and had a full cup. We had to wake them up. Even the few sips of the potion had powered me into such a deep, relaxed state that I could not now move my body. Even in sleep, I could feel this. I was afraid.

I saw the shadows of men in the doorway.

"Nightmares," the Amantile spirit said.

It was a nightmare as the two men snuck into the room to look upon half-naked girls.

"No, Nightmare!" said Amantile. Words, it seemed, were ever difficult for plants. It showed me in images what he meant. I saw the story nearly as clearly as the Twisted Flower had shown.

After he helped me out of my body, we stumbled around the room in spirit form, helping hold each other up. I was unused to such travel, and he stumbled on roots that were poor substitutes for feet.

Thefare stood by the doorway, but Pesne was clearly making use of this opportunity. He moved around the room, looking at our bodies in the veil-like shifts. The images were confused. I felt a hand begin to touch my body while we looked for one girl whose body did not care for the root.

I saw her first. "There."

I felt bad for the girl, but I supported Amantile as his spirit hands mingled into her brain, using the potent potion already in her system to speed its power to where her mind disagreed with the effects. Nauseated by his act, I turned my head. To see Pesne by my bed.

The girl woke up screaming, and I slammed back into my body. I woke with a shuddering gasp. I was grateful to be awake, more because I could still feel the warmth of a man's hand on my breast.

The men made a hasty retreat.

Velia came rushing into the room and screamed as she saw their backs. She turned to me with a look of horror, and then to the girl now gulping down air, still trying to scream. I watched as Velia turned from a horrified woman into not just a healer's wife, but a woman of women's art with a near audible clap.

The plant spirit was still making the girl so terrified that her screaming woke others, and more women came into the room.

The ensuing confusion made it clear: they needed a Doctor-Diviner. The girls were weak and began to vomit. Velia was out of her depth and began to look frantic. I made my way slowly to her—slowly was about all I could do.

"Do you know the symbols for this troubled dreaming?" I asked.

She trembled, looking as if I might just have tacitly accused her of dosing us unwillingly. She clenched her jaw, stood up straight, but admitted she did not.

Speaking with effort, her jaw still so tight, her words and mouth clipped with anger. "How could Deeta make the tea so strong?" she asked me.

"Perhaps she brewed it too long, or added too much, misunderstanding your instruction?"

I could see the doubt enter her mind as quickly as mine

did. It had been intentional. For Pesne, I could only assume.

"You know the symbols better than I. And…" she hesitated, "and… the antidote?"

"I'll need my bag," I said. "And some clothes!"

I felt too naked in only this thin shift and grabbed what clothes I could find. I asked a servant woman for a bowl of water and used the blessed coolness to wash my face. I helped the girls as best I could. They were too dizzy to vomit into bowls on their own. Without enough servants, and certainly Arntlei and Ati weren't present, some of the girls heaved onto the floor, their beds, even their laps, their long hair trailing into the mess. Servants came in and cleaned up as quickly as they could.

From what I could tell, none of the other girls knew that the men had come to see us. Apparently, and I did not know how grateful I should be for this, only Velia and I had seen the men's retreat.

When my bag came, I painted the girl with symbols to banish her nightmares. While the other girls finished vomiting, I let them drink clean water. Calmly, with the appearance of ritual, I made them all take drops of a tincture that would combat the nausea, and then sip a potent antidote to the Amantile. With as much show as I could manage, I had us all join in in support of the girl's nightmare lingering in the room.

In Ndeb, I thanked the Amantile for his help, and yet also banished him, sending his spirit back to the roots still growing out in nature, doing what I could, though I was still struggling with his potent sleep, to help him find his way.

That done, I sang a soothing song for the girls. I used a small gourd to tap out the beat of a healing lullaby. The tense energy of the room slowly faded, and the girls, reasonably tired with the excitement of the evening, also started to sleep.

When they were asleep, I finished dressing in some of my real clothes, putting on my apprentice robe over the awful riot of color, travel-stained though the hem clearly was. I shoved the rest of my clothes into the bag. I sat on my bed to put on my sturdy walking boots, tying the laces firmly.

I went to where Velia was still standing. I had her follow me out the door.

"Velia, what were they thinking?" I whispered.

"What do you mean?" she said, turning away from me.

"The Amantile in the tea," I said. "I only had two sips, but it was too strong. Just with that, I could not wake. What would have happened to little Nerinai, or even Hastia, who had a full cup?"

I saw the muscles in her jaw working. She did not look at me, but blood drained from her face. She waved her hands before her eyes, closing them, brushing away the thoughts that her friends might have betrayed her.

She whispered finally, so softly it was as if they came from the bottom trace of her lungs and still faded from a journey of such length, "For the men? For Pesne? But why?"

I threw up my hands. "It was foolish!" I paused. "And dangerous. I hope you will let them know that." I started to walk away.

"Do not tell Tages," she said, with her hand on my arm, stopping me.

I turned on her angrily. "Why not?"

"Pesne wanted to see his bride and all else she would bring."

"Bring? There were unmarried women and *girls* in this

room. Could he not have picked a better time?" I shuddered. I knew how I'd felt when I realized Ravantha had watched me bathe. Knowing a man had looked upon me, touched me, when I was vulnerable was, in fact, worse.

Poor Hastia, marrying a man willing to participate in such a thing.

I felt a sudden shock as another thought formed in my brain. "He's claiming more than Hastia in his negotiations?"

Velia shrugged. "He likes women."

"You are saying he's not content with merely one wife?"

"He is not looking for more than one wife, but women to serve him." Velia's eyes moved as she pondered all we'd seen. "I think... perhaps... Thefare..." She looked up at me with some faint sense of assurance. "Thefare must have claimed you as a niece, even illegitimate. Ravantha certainly hasn't kept silent. The Westvell people call you by her name, not Sen of the Woods."

I shook my head. "Velia, why did you help him? To do the fete?"

"Yes, I brought you here by his request. He'd gifted me handsomely for organizing this fete. I..." Her lips turned into a line, and she drew a ragged breath through her nose. "I didn't think... think more on this."

"I'm going home. Keep an eye on the little ones. I'll make more of the antidote, and something to help those who might remain sick for days."

She nodded. Her expression was bleak.

I turned and made my way out.

"Don't tell Tages!" she called out to me, but made no move to stop me.

I had to pass through Thefare's great hall. There were men

there, presumably awakened by the commotion. Thefare and Pesne were joined by Larce, and several of the other men who had been dancing with the women.

"Ah, Sen. You helped calm the excitement with the women?" Thefare asked.

"As is my duty to my mentor. They will rest more peacefully now," I said. Having seen in my sleep vision men wanting to see half-naked girls, I added, "They will sleep light, however." It was a lie. "The girl's nightmare put them on edge, even while I banished it."

Thefare nodded, and with a gesture sent most of the men away. Shock was still plain on Larce's face as he finally recognized me. I could still feel the paint, stiff on my face. My clothes were now a mockery of the costume I wore earlier under my usual adept garb. He did not leave the room with the others, staying near the exit.

I was near the archway to the exit when Thefare said, "Stay a moment, Sen."

I hefted my shoulder bag and turned only my head toward him. "Yes, my lord?"

From the corner of my eyes, I could see Larce crossing his arms to hide how he'd bowed up to defend me. He stepped back, his jaw clenched.

Thefare turned to the other man. "Lord Pesne, this is my brother's daughter. Now you can see her without all that finery. She will come with Hastia as part of her dowry."

Pesne took a step toward me. I stopped him with a gesture.

"You are mistaken," I said firmly. My hand held before me was probably rude—dismissive even, to this rich lord. I did not care. "I am an adept Doctor-Diviner, student of the great Tages."

"You are a comely lass. Lovelier than your sister," Pesne said as if what I'd just said didn't matter.

"Hastia is not my sister. I would be wary, sir, about your dealings. This man had no value for me till months ago. There was a child he rightly assumed was dead till he decided I *might* be her because of a passing familiarity with the baby's mother." I paused. "Hastia is a good woman, so there's no need to make use of an *unproven* lineage to sweeten the pot. Pointless, as well, as I'm legally bound to the Doctor-Diviner Tages."

"Your skills would make you the more worth having," Pesne said. "Before you were only a servant to your sister. All you brought then was your body, which I do not fault."

I was astonished by his complete disregard for my statements. It was as if my status meant nothing, as if his agreement with Thefare were far more legal than the one already binding Tages and me.

"You will not have me. Thefare cannot speak for me. Only Tages can."

"His wife already has and has been compensated," Thefare said with a grin. His look said that I was worth less because I might be a bastard. An unproven lineage did not matter. It was better, in fact. No one could claim me. Though clearly, they had.

I knew this to be a lie. A lie compounding the greed-filled deceit toward Velia.

Bile rose to my throat. I remembered that hand on my breast, even though I'd not fully felt it in that stupor of Amantile. I was enraged.

Both brothers were terrible. If I could have, I'd have gone down to the vaults and gotten Thielle's broken necklace, and marched straight to Ravantha and put it into her own hands—even if I were to hang for theft. I was that infuriated.

"I am no servant!" I trembled knowing that even if I had been, I still wouldn't deserve such despicable attention. "I am not subject to either of you. My allegiance is only to Doctor-Diviner Tages."

I turned and walked out the door, despite being called back. Larce was in the passageway, concealed behind the open door, which he slammed shut. I had no real faith in this man's friendship with Ravantha, but he had his hand on the shut door, visibly working not to go through the door and smash heads. His entire body was vibrating.

In that moment, I realized that while his friendship with Marce might be the truest and purest he had, his feelings for others might be quite complex, even divided. He turned to look at me, and I could see the pain deepening the lines on his still-young face. He moved as soon as I started to walk away and stopped me.

"What do you want?"

"The rumor is true," Larce said. "Thefare offered you as part of the dowry for his niece, like you were some bauble or jewel, or one of the fifty head of prize cattle he added to the pot."

"Legally, he can't, unless Tages agreed—which he would not." I shook my head. "I'm going to Tages."

"Sen, what happened? You were already upset before that exchange."

"We were given a sleeping potion. The Amantile did not agree with one of the women and inspired a nightmare."

"Hence the screaming. Wait, why were you given a sleeping potion?"

"There are other reasons for girls to wake up screaming. So, feel free to guess."

I hadn't thought he could get angrier. If the wall hadn't been stone, I think he might have punched it. However, something I said had caused a transformation I could see on Larce's face. He'd gone from—I thought—real concern about my welfare, to contemplative. It was a contemplation marred by an awful gleam in his eye. So caught by his thoughts, he forgot about me. He fell back, turned, and went to some other portion of the castle I did not know. I did not care. I did not care that I would be traveling at night, when lions tended to hunt.

I had other ways to travel, but I didn't want Jackal's Way. I was too angry. I'd have punched any lion if it too tried to violate my body with teeth or claws. The handprint on my breast still hotter than my comparatively cooler body.

I walked fast. I had to know whether Tages had known about me being part of Hastia's bride portion.

Chapter Nine

I watched Tages in his study for a long while. He was completely absorbed with my notes and writing his own notes in the journal he used for his own observations. It was some comfort to me to see that he had value for my work, which he could not do if he'd let me be taken away.

During my walk back, I'd realized much of the fete, the women's side of it, had been designed by Velia. However surprised or horrified she'd been, she might still be glad to have me gone. I knew that she had loved every minute of the fete, despite noticing the lines on my chin, or the colors of my gowns denoting me as Hastia's property. Even before that evening had started, I'd seen how she had chafed a long time, not because of me, but because of her husband. Because she dreamed of more.

Velia wanted more than what this distracted scholar might give her. Not but two, maybe even one generation before, she'd probably have had it—equal to value and respect as her husband could expect. Even while that was fading in this new age of science, her own son now had more status because of his studies. Tages could easily do with refreshed renown, going beyond what he had been teaching, creating a more profitable career in a university, rather than rusticating here.

Helping Aranthur, perhaps, or if he could actually move to Jambrone, where he could teach, might offer that opportunity. As he couldn't help Aranthur, he could become a professor at the university. It would suit him far better than all this solitude. Thinking of Gavius, I knew that he'd have more than letters, but conversations that would get him away from his desk and invigorate his research.

There, Velia might have something of value also. It might be new, and it certainly wouldn't be betrayed by those she had trusted as friends and family.

How galling must it be to see the rites and women's festivities she was so good at being turned into a mockery of their former glory?

Shame burned me in that summer night, worse than the memory of Pesne's hand upon my breast as I slept. It made the night seem almost cool. I'd left her alone to cope with all that. She'd spent days, I was sure, prepping all that return to former glory—a splendid celebration of women—to have it so easily torn apart by terrible men, aided by Arntlei and Ati.

An image came to me of Velia as fulfilled as I've ever seen her. She glowed, helping the girls and women get ready for this fete. How she must miss the community of women that had once been her daily fare before marriage. Now rare! Worse, there were no fine clothes, no fashion that she clearly, if secretly, loved, no whispers in the night of women's mysteries, fewer friends. Not if Ati and Arntlei were her choices.

Adept

Velia was stuck associating with, currently, two people who cared so little for that life that it must have felt as if we ignored her. Daily, especially after the son she'd doted on left for the university, Tages and I had become more absorbed in our studies. We left her to be, and feel more than alone.

I felt bile rise to my throat as I thought of my own tacit betrayal. I'd learned so much from her and had taken it for granted. She might not have introduced me to the more private and sacred aspects of midwifery, but she had taught me a great deal about it regardless.

I stepped back to think a moment. It was late, and I did not want to disturb him. I lay on the floor by the kitchen fire and rested till morning, but without sleep. I was too worried about what would happen when Velia came home. Morning rituals of breaking the night's fast gave me some insight into Velia's choices.

My initial plans for making a small meal showed me that there was little to eat.

Surprised, I went about the room, looking at the bins of food stores, and what bounty we might have had from the garden. I understood a little bit better. I shook my head. In some ways, what else was the woman to do when he did not go out to heal people and used what money he gained to buy books and equipment?

He was a grown man. Velia should be his partner, his colleague, his wife—not some servant to easily dismiss to the background of dust, dirt, and decay. That's what a new apprentice could be for. I certainly had done my share of house cleaning, cooking, washing, and gardening as an apprentice.

More: I thought of the times, so many, many times, she'd actually asked for that. The irritating tone of that bickering background noise suddenly shifted in my mind, my ears hearing the memory of those requests as desperation. Her own observations of their household life, akin to any divination Tages might have been proud of.

For weeks I'd been gone, stopping only to drop off plants and get orders. I had not been here either to help her in her daily chores he'd long been sluffing off, or to observe what was happening.

I put something together for my master and myself. I put the food by his elbow, but his absorption in his reading was still too great. Even if his reading lamp had nearly burnt all its oil, sunrise offered its fresh supply of light. He barely noticed me.

He looked so thin. I wondered when he'd eaten last. The food I'd given him that morning, if he'd forgotten that bowl in his absorption, what was I to do about it?

Neither an apprentice nor adept will ever get the income the master would. Tages had not ventured out as much as I had, since he'd sent me on the rounds he'd once made. Perhaps he'd channeled the growing loss of his divinatory insight into all this study. His messy desk, a talisman against despair.

I recognized some of the bounty from my labors sent on by grateful and conscientious villagers. It was not, however, the degree of wealth even Cai had brought, and when Tages still ventured out.

Velia had her own resources, but it was not enough. And what Tages's one student brought in did not add much.

The pile of books had grown. Looking at that, and the books spilling out of bookshelves, I wondered how much of that wealth had been diverted to books that would further her husband's studies. He'd refused to be tempted by the city—though he'd embraced it in his own way with books and equipment, which only limited her even more. What she understood, she despised.

This wasn't a true thought. She had complained. And I'd rather that undercurrent of tension than all this distracted scholarship.

I sat down on a pile of books in a chair. I remembered she'd once been as lively as Cai, Aule, Tages, and myself discussing herbs, tinctures, anatomy—especially women's bodies. Somehow, even her beloved son, Aule, had joined in this slow dismissal of her art and magic in favor of science. Sweat cooled on my skin as I realized how much I myself had contributed to this.

If I were gone, maybe Tages would *have* to travel again—old, though he was—and she could imagine that he would return her to the life she most likely remembered, and could and should expect. Months ago, Cai told me, even before he'd gained his Mastery scar, that life was change.

Hers could never return to what it was, what it must have been, even were she to leave.

I ate and then stood up and went to my hut, which I had not seen yet. I had come home and been happily distracted by discussions and gardening with Tages. I might have been scrubbed clean the day before, but my travel clothes were not fresh, and I despised the finery I'd worn from the castle and slept in. I had clean clothes in my hut and wanted to change out of the strange mixture of finery and travel-stained clothes.

On the threshold, power hit me in the face, stopping me before I could enter the room.

Chapter Ten

Velia had painted my one-room hut. Bespelled it, rather. In the room lit by sunlight, it was clear. In the dark, I might not have noticed. I stood in the doorway and critiqued it.

Poor thing. She had, for lack of a better word, spelled the symbols wrong in places. The intent was clear. It confirmed all my speculations.

I turned back to the main house and knocked loudly on the study's archway.

Tages turned, startled.

"Yes?"

"I think you had better see this," I said. I picked up the bowl of congealed stew beside his elbow and forced him to look at it. I wasn't going to reheat it all over again. "Eat first. Then come see. It will wait."

He ate with a grimace, but something in my face made him finish. He then followed me. He did not hesitate on the threshold.

"Wait," I cried out.

He shook his head. "Don't worry, my dear. It's not for me."

I pointed at a cluster of symbols.

"Well, maybe that part," he said, "but not in a way that would bind me." His tone was light, but his expression grim. It was a painful part of the spell. It used his natural obliviousness, his focus, to have him let Velia put this spell in motion.

He read the whole set, the various colors of white, red, and black, and their other tones for symbolic clarity.

For someone who had bedecked herself in most of the modern fashions just the night before, it was a bit of a contrast. This was a strange mixture of old symbolic language as used on some of the older households, including hers, which her cousin lived in. There was also Ndeb, or an attempt at it.

Written on the walls, there was an implication of Tages's inattention in Ndeb with a three-footed green symbol under a circle, vertically split in two with green and orange that implied his age and waning years.

I could see how her magic must have understood his growing blindness, but it stumbled. However much women's work had magic, Velia's midwifery tilted toward the practical. She tried, but couldn't say it. Perhaps she didn't know, but only guessed what he'd told me himself at the end of spring.

In poorly written Ndeb, she implied I was causing his madness. Divided from him was a symbol of my obedience to her, with an older woman's need to teach or guide the younger. An inverted triangle, one under the other. All lost opportunities there, since the day I came.

I was also written into a symbol of Hastia's marriage, like a bride price of cattle. So, she had known, but maybe not so repulsively as what Thefare had made use of.

Instead of listing the number of cattle, I was clearly the diamond in virgin colors, along with a smaller one of a girl child, Casiea, within the gold and blue triangles of her marriage. Some of the symbols, and possibly paint from the same pots, had been drawn on my face—including the double lines of service.

It was, actually, just *one* of her options. Mastery, my own marriage, moving to live with Ravantha, going back to Grandmother Turani's cave grotto, and even being attacked by jackals. Each as elaborate as the next. She'd thrown all these ideas against the wall, hoping one would stick.

He sighed and came to sit in the sunlight. His shoulders were slumped as if he carried all her cheeses to the market on his shoulders in one go. Something he'd never done, of course.

"Poor Velia. I had not realized how much she counted on me. And how much she blames *you* for my distraction."

"Couldn't you have another or many other apprentices?"

"Of course! But none would be as fluent in Ndeb as you," he said.

I shook my head, thinking, *What? Isn't that what you would teach them?* My disgust was already choking me, and he continued past my shock. *What a horrible excuse.*

"They'd not be as skilled and interested, and you came to me at a time when science echoed my own studies." His eyes gleamed like a man in love at the memory—not with me, but his work. "Fate and timing were against her. And she has made this against you."

He turned to look at me. For a long moment, he examined me with his healer eyes. He wiped some white paint from my face. "You came from the castle, and something has distressed you."

"The man Thefare has been negotiating with, Pesne,

apparently likes women." I hesitated to say more, because it was more awful than I could bear at the moment.

"Sen, it is already appalling. Tell me all. I cannot fix a disease with a lack of detail on the extent of the symptoms. There's plenty noted here already," he said, gesturing toward my hut.

I nodded and allowed the near hysteria of the spelling to reach my thinking. How frantic she must have been to do it when he would not notice.

With a deep breath, I told him what had happened.

"They used her, her eagerness for women's ritual and ceremony, and her understanding of herbs. I think they even made use of her secret wish laid bare here."

I kept to Thefare's betrayal, and Ati's probable one, as it was her servant who'd brewed the Amantile so strong. "Velia probably knew that the young women and girls needed something calming after all their excitement. I can attest, they'd probably have stayed awake throughout the night talking otherwise. But Velia did not know Thefare's plans."

I didn't tell him of my work with the Amantile. That actually wasn't important, in the face of things.

I laid thick the betrayals his wife experienced, adding to his burden. If he—a husband, a Doctor-Diviner—had paid proper attention to Velia, none of it would have happened.

All he said was, "You are a bound adept."

I gestured to my hut. "This is grief," I said.

"Yes. It is powered by her emotions. You might have been snared by this, at least for a time, had you slept here when you returned, instead of coming a day late, and working with me and caring for the new plants, and going over books," he said.

"Is she that good? Think of that... spelling of maiden." The sacerdotal script of Ndeb had been written from the basic symbology of the geometric patterns. I looked at the walls anew, as if I were venturing into Jackal's Way. Similar to speaking with Twisted Flower or Amantile, I now could see that there was as much power as I'd thought. It hadn't been Velia's magic that had struck me so powerfully, but her emotions. I could all but hear her internal rage and despair.

"Well, perhaps not. There are clearly weaknesses."

We said nothing about the deep wrong in this. Causing illness—to a person or community—was more than a deep social error. I could see it as a symptom of deep hurt.

I thought back to my apprentice days when I might—but thankfully didn't—say something unforgivable to Ravantha about her rape in a reaction against something she'd said. Over the past many weeks, how often had I reacted to something someone said, steeped in their own misery or fear?

Yet, as we sat in the sunlight, I knew we both thought of the illness we were bound to cure. I wondered if he knew what kind of Medicine he would have to employ here. I bowed my head, having a good idea that paying attention to his wife might not last long. It was the cure. Easiest to hand. With a sigh, I looked at the reality. His work dominated his thoughts.

My pity for her grew. Velia might have tried everything else in her power to talk to her husband for quite some time—and been ignored. Not only by him, but by their son, and his students. How many times had she tried to get his attention to her distress, and he remained oblivious—the *one* man who ought to have paid attention by right of their marriage and love, as well as his chosen profession.

I could feel my nose get red, and tears rim my eyes. This magic—poorly done as it was— was never intended to do anything but what it did: get her husband's attention. It was the act of a deeply unhappy woman.

I had expected that one day my own life might be filled with books, rotting apple cores, beakers and burners, and endless, endless study. At what cost?

A wife, a companion turned servant? What came first? The fading of second sight, or the growing obsession with scholarship, with science? The loss of his insight seemed paired with his distinct lack of observation.

Maybe I was extremely lucky he'd found me under the Tree he couldn't see, and used that as a means to give me my adept scars —while still unable to see my own ancestors.

As we sat in silence and no doubt both thought these things in our different ways and perspectives, I realized that Velia had joined in the powerful threads that had begun to weave around me since spring.

How much of his ability to divine is gone? I wondered. I could but venture a question.

"Will you divine something for me? It's not just Velia I'm concerned about, but Ravantha and Thefare. I think they both have used her, and her discontent, in different ways."

"Yes, Velia did press Ravantha's suit to me, even while I contemplated your visits without her influence. What is it that you would have me divine?"

"What is happening with those threads of tension along the border? How strong are they becoming? Rope, or is it just embroidery?"

"I am at fault. You told me of your concerns long ago, you

wrote me notes so I'd have your observations to hand, and letters when your travels kept you too far. I put them aside to read in more depth later, to focus on the lymphatic system and the circulatory system. I never read those letters in greater detail. I never took the time to use the threshing basket, the only ritual of divination I still have. I have just had a powerful lesson in my indifference to matters of importance outside my workroom. You are right. We must learn something more of what is going on. Come along."

He gathered up his round basket of symbols and the threshing basket that had only ever been used for divination. He did not speak to me, but walked to the little clearing between his house and my hut. He poured the symbols into the threshing basket and then shook it, the way any woman threshing grain might have done, separating the chaff from the grain.

In this case, Tages threshed lies from the truth.

He looked at what came to the top, and then did it again. He repeated this action for a while. Studying the symbols. He was silent, and I did not ask questions.

In my own understanding of this work, it was a matter of concentration that helped one see not only the importance of the symbols that came to the top, but the thought one put into it. There was a degree of attention one had to apply for the critical interpretation and explanation of the whole reading.

Knowing Tages, he was examining the symbols with as much attention as he would give when dissecting an animal that had died of some disease or disorder. He had to know what had happened on the inside, to know how they had reflected the disorder with symptoms observable on the outside.

He finally set the basket down and sat on a bench. He was

still deep in thought. I waited.

Finally, he stood, gathered up the symbols from the basket, and set things back the way they were before his work, saying words over them to clear the energies the divining had brought forth.

"What did you see from what I have done?" he asked.

"I did not see the symbols, Master."

"Understood, but there are times you are sensitive to energy."

I shrugged. "I'm perhaps too upset to notice anything. But... I did feel a sense of comfort, as if a child again in Grandmother Turani's arms. It was, however, as if she were protecting me from a great deal of harm. I also felt as if I would be fine, despite the upcoming battles."

"Interesting," he said. "You echo some of what I read that cheered me."

"The rest was confused." I paused, thinking of how to phrase what I had felt. "While some of it felt familiar as the subjects in those letters, I could not tell if that was because I was already thinking about those things, or if the confusion came because some of the greater images were completely outside my experience."

"You are young yet," he said. "You'll be pleased to know that Fuluns will return sometime today."

"That does not please me."

"I'll grant you that," he said with a wry grin. It turned to gravity as he said, "If you are brave enough to join me, I must make Thefare aware that you are *not* free by *my* choice!" He paused and took my hands. He looked at my white adept scar and where my Mastery scar would one day be. "I had thought to give you your Mastery this week." His face showed real distress. "You are doing the work adeptly, and had before I gave you the first mark. But it seems as if I must protect you a while, again, and a little longer from the machinations of these men."

I hung my head, so he could not see the grimace on my face.

There was no actual reason for him to offer me my Mastery, much less take it away. It was a carrot on a stick as if I were some mulish mule. And I knew it. For one, I'd not done all the study or work required. I'd not once divined anything. He'd be a fool to let go of an adept, considering the circumstances we'd just witnessed. I barely hid my disgust. I bowed my shoulders as there was this whole castle fiasco to cope with. I needed to brush this aside.

The great Doctor-Diviner Tages's reputation might be enough to protect me. While he had some respect from universities up north, clearly that standing had tarnished in his own country.

I couldn't help but remember Ravantha calling him a "glorified apothecary," along with Larce's brutal assessment of the scales of weights of power.

I nodded. "I am willing to join you," I said. "Let me clean myself up first." I could still feel stiffened paint along my hairline in places, pulling at any expression. My clothes were still travel and gardening-stained, and stunk, mingled with the repulsive gauze of finery. "You need a wash too, Master," I added.

I cleaned my hut's walls, roughly, just to erase Velia's deep sorrows. Then I bathed myself.

I knew I was stalling. I dreaded what we were about to do.

Chapter Eleven

However much Tages assumed he could still protect me, I realized that he was also holding onto me. With or without a carrot dangling in front of me. My regret was that I no longer wished to study the same way. It hurt like a bone-deep bruise.

Tages needed me to do the work of an adept, because while the villagers' payments and gifts were smaller, they still filled his coffers and allowed him to do the work he'd yearned to do all his life. He wasn't aware he might starve if he did that. Velia had cared for him too well as to run the household with such efficiency to where she also became somehow unnoticed... even unseen.

Maybe he hadn't sent me off to do his proper work merely to test me, or to use me, but so he could pursue his studies without interruption. Yet if he could dismiss his obligations to Velia, he certainly didn't need to send me away to do so. I'd have joined in, most probably. My travels must have given me some perspective. He'd spent his whole life, especially the last several months, creating the laboratory and the network of scholars he needed to do the work he desired to do. I could not begrudge him the study.

I loved it as well. I had just learned I wanted something else. As we walked, I wiped away several tears.

As much as I wanted to continue my own study, I also wanted to do what I had been doing: give aid to people. Comfort them, and heal their wounds and illnesses both physically and spiritually. As an adept, I was bound by his choice and direction, rather than my own. He was a master, and I hoped I still had plenty to learn.

For the first time, I wanted to leave his tutelage.

There was marvelous temptation to leave right then, if only to avoid any difficult scenes we'd meet at the castle. Of the people who seemed to think they could make any choices for my life, he was the only one with the authority to do so. It broke my heart to realize I was chafing under that authority, even while I had decided reasons to be glad of it!

Gavius, and maybe a few others, might have read the book I'd coauthored. Reviewing past events as we walked, I thought about the conversation with Larce. Titles meant power and reputations, and clearly, Doctor-Diviners could easily be scorned by those who patronized them. I understood when it was done to Bathos or Thucer, but *Tages*? It was a shock.

The previous night's events had proved just that. I was walking toward the lion's den again, and my protection was thin indeed. I nearly turned back, yet again.

We arrived at the castle. Before we'd left, Tages had helped ensure that all signs of the other night's costume and paint were gone—to ensure that none of Velia's misguided magic lingered on me. I hadn't told Tages the spells were weak tea indeed. I couldn't betray Velia; she'd had more than enough of that already.

We arrived a scant hour after Fuluns made his triumphant return. He made my skin crawl. He wasn't handsome, and while he was slighter than his brother, pride seemed to linger in his movements and gestures, giving him a weight and presence his brother lacked.

He was still showing off one of his finds from his trade-making travels. No one took note of us, eager to see what he was trying to display. Tages and I looked at each other.

"Isn't that a…" I reached for the words useful in Ndeb, but had to stick to Obrone, and so whispered them. "A muzzle-loaded snaplock firearm? Didn't we read about this in one of Aule's books?" I asked Tages in Ndeb.

"Yes. Describing damage done when the device is misused, as it easily can be when one mixes metal and fire—as any idiot studying alchemy might learn, even without the more refined study of chemistry."

Of course. Chemistry. Which was why Aule had written about this kind of weapon. Chemistry included things like gunpowder and fireworks.

"Or when its projectile connects with the victim. The damage is said to be worse than an arrow," I said.

Aule remained his father and mother's son, because despite whatever eagerness for things that exploded, he sent diagrams of potential damage as well for the two healers in his family, three if he'd included me. The layered medical diagram had made the extent of damage… quite clear. Those drawings displayed the damage one of this variety of weapons could do—to both the intended target, as well as the user.

Tages nodded and said, still in Ndeb, "Fuluns is

propitiating his ancestor."

"Relative," I corrected, nodding to Thefare. "That one lives."

Tages smirked. "He wishes the goodwill of those who are powerful," he said. "As many do, and we have learned today."

I tried not to laugh. The look on Fuluns's face was clear. "There is a smell of acrid smoke," I replied, still in Ndeb. "Do you think they fired the gun?"

"I do not know," Tages said, ever focused on observable details.

Thefare noticed us and called us forward. "Come! You must see this new invention my brother has brought back. It is a matchlock."

"Newer than a snaplock? I have heard of these things," Tages said.

"You are interested in new ideas, from what I understand," Thefare said.

"New inventions to help me and my student study how to return people to health, yes. Inventions that render grievous injury or death for user or victim, I find a bit more... unfortunate. At least we are prepared to heal both victim and the user of damage incurred by these *inaccurate* weapons," he said, undermining any glory the thing had on its own.

Thefare and Fuluns looked at each other as if Tages were predictable, and less worthy.

"I did not come," Tages said, "to see the gifts your brother brings. I came to discuss my adept."

"Ah. Brought her back, I see. Hastia will be glad."

Tages shook his head. "I do not know what my wife has said or arranged, but she had no authority to do so. My adept is bound to *me* a while longer. She is not free to go where she wishes. The work she does is still at my command. If you defy this, you put at risk *all* contracts of masters with their apprentices, adepts, or journeymen."

I saw Thefare's jaw clench with temper. The point I'd tried to use laid bare. "You would gain more income from sending her off with Hastia than from her traveling to aid the villages," Thefare countered with some heat.

Tages shook his head. "Clearly, Velia has discussed wealth, but I measure my adept's worth not in money or trade. I measure it in her knowledge and learning—not only in what strange plants she brings me, but in what she learns from what she does, as well as the hours we spend discussing our work. She will one day *surpass* me as a Doctor-Diviner, and this scheme would prevent that good work from benefiting the land!"

I had not known he saw me in this light. I was surprised that he felt this way. Was it true? How gilded was that carrot he'd dangled in front of me only a few hours earlier?

Fuluns had been staring at me. "She does look like Ravantha," he said. "So, you are my daughter?"

"Ravantha's child was exposed. No one claimed her. Not Ravantha, not Rasce, not Thefare, not Fuluns. I was found and claimed as a daughter by Grandmother Turani, who arranged for me to study with Tages when she was dying," I said, feeling bold. Tages smiled at me. He'd heard the choice of my words.

"Does that matter? You're alive and here," Fuluns said, dismissive. "And I claim you now, and will do what I want with you. Give you to my daughter's intended, and be done with the whole lot."

I felt a rush of fury, but Tages sighed expressively, so I did not speak. I looked down at the matchlock firearm. There was an oil lamp nearby for the gloom of that side of the room, and a match exposed to air. It was near the firearm. I wondered how familiar Fuluns was with the firearm. They were not widely used, or even well-known. Clearly, he had little idea of how to use one of these things—or even how dangerous they could be.

"It does matter," Tages said. "There's no proof she's your daughter, Fuluns. You cannot claim a girl as yours because you like the looks of her. As I am her master, and she already has the scars of an adept, she is under my protection. The laws of the land demand that this contract be respected."

I muttered the words of heat and fire in Ndeb, so low that even Tages could not hear them. The match was close enough to others that it set off the other matches, which ignited the flash pan. The firearm jumped with a bang just as he thumped his staff down to emphasize the import of his words.

Fuluns leaped back, as did his brother and others in the room.

Tages did not jump. He had too much iron resolve. This was the teacher I respected. Not the scholar with greasy hair and a pile of dust and cobwebs on his shoulders. His white knuckles were the only indication of surprise he felt when the bang overtook the sound of his staff hitting the stone floor.

In Ndeb, he whispered, "Foolish girl! You do not play with these energies!"

"I'm sorry!" I said, without any remorse, especially when I realized he was trying not to grin.

Together we cleared the smoke away, and in his Ndeb words of air and wind, he admitted, "Well, at least they believe I'm serious about this."

"I hope so."

Thefare recovered more quickly than his brother. "Well, it is good to know the thing works, but as for you, this is the second negotiation someone of Rasce's blood has attempted to thwart."

"She's not of Rasce's blood, by Ravantha or anyone!" Tages said firmly and loudly enough to project around the room.

Tages held my arm tightly, as if he were about to pull me back and leave. He was stopping me from saying that it was Fuluns who had ruined those negotiations.

"My adept has *nothing* to do with your negotiations," Tages said. "Nor does her master. If you will send a messenger to my wife, that she must come home, I will leave you in peace."

Thefare looked at Tages, who was clearly angry.

"Well, it pleases me that you will do what you can to control your household!" He snapped his fingers and sent a messenger off. "As you are here, I will make use of you both. You will tend to the burns of some of my guards," he said with a dismissive wave. "As is your duty."

"What happened?" Tages asked, ignoring the imperious gesture.

"A fire in the guardroom," he said. "An event that insulted not one of my guests, but two!"

We couldn't understand what that meant. He'd turned his back on us. We learned more from the guards we tended, who weren't badly burned. Servants were already cleaning up the mess, and other guards grumbled at having to scour the walls and floors of the treasure room. Thefare was going to assess the greater damage when it was clean. Among other things, Pesne's contract had been damaged, as well as the seeds he'd brought to sweeten the pot.

Larce had gone off in a huff in his burnt and smoke-damaged finery, as he'd been insulted not only from losing in a card game with some of the guards, but that his ale had been poisoned by whoever set the fire—leaving them all to fall asleep and nearly get roasted by the fire. Pesne had been just as offended that his seed and his contract had been burned, and it was taking some consoling on Thefare's part. With evil smirks and laughter, the guards implied that it wasn't Thefare, but women, who were doing the consoling.

At that ribald intimation, still infuriated by what he'd learned, Tages pulled me away, as I gave a final rub of burn cream on one guard's legs. He was grim and silent, holding onto my arm at every turn.

Outside the walls of Thefare's town, when we were on the road back to his little compound, Tages finally spoke. Jackal seemed to be pacing us a little distance from the road.

"This is worse than I thought," he said.

"What do you mean?"

"The divination mentioned this, but I did not understand it. There is greater danger to you now than I interpreted. I should have examined your notes and letters better! You were clear about the tensions along the Westvell and Thefarland borders. You noted much of what I see now, and you noted it while it was in its infancy. I'll admit, I thought I had time, but I spent much of it on my studies. Do you see what I see, not only from divination, but in the ill energies that have spread throughout the land?"

It was clear he had missed something, and he was coming face-to-face with it. It was not up to me to downplay the truth of that difficult realization.

"I'm as bad as Bathos," he muttered.

I thought for a moment, letting the rhythm of our footfalls echo my heartbeat, and looked at the world with my Doctor-Diviner's eyes—and those that Jackal had taught me. I could feel it in the ground and in the air.

Maybe because Jackal, like all predators, killed with teeth, tasking flesh and blood, there was a metallic smell of blood. The visions moved from some golden-amber glow into a red that burned toward black. It filled my head, making it hurt enough to include nausea.

"There's a battle coming," I said, "with more than swords and arrows, but with a few firearms even Fuluns doesn't know how to use, though he brought them." I swallowed spittle that welled in my mouth, but couldn't take the taste of blood from it, as if I'd bitten my tongue. Jackal laughed.

"I am glad you see it, too."

"Do you really think there will be a real war? A real battle? There hasn't been anything like that in generations, am I not right? We don't study much history, unless it has something to do with medical science, but actual war?"

"No. It is rare. And it may still be stopped, if I can get a letter through our contacts in Jambrone to someone with far more authority than—well—the land chiefs involved." He shook his head. "It is clear that there is more going on than any kind of battle. I must get you to safety," he said.

"Where?"

"Ravantha's manor. She will stop little short of murder to protect you."

I was about to say that I would feel far more trapped in her household than not, especially as she was certainly involved in the coming war. She was building an army with her people. However, as far as I was concerned, the word *overprotective* could easily describe her. "But what about her army?" I began to ask, but Tages interrupted me with a question of his own.

"How often do you do that?" he asked, interrupting me, and what I was about to say. "Play with energies, and cause things to happen?"

"Only a few times. I spooked a horse. I promise that I had no intention of setting off the gun *quite* so explosively. The matches I did not see as clearly were set off, which added to the oil and gunpowder."

"No, you weren't there when Aule showed his precious few matches to me. I have clearly other means of lighting a fire at need."

"I didn't even create that one from scratch, if you are curious. The oil lamp was..."

He laughed. "Too close! And the way people were milling about, you actually prevented greater injury."

"At the cost of a scorched table and the rising heartbeat of many people."

We grinned at each other, and then continued on as our smiles faded. We were both disquieted. In the silence of the day, I realized I had both my teachers with me. Tages to the right, Jackal to the left, blood on his teeth, exposed in a wicked grin. I found no comfort in either, but glad of their protective company all the same.

Chapter Twelve

⟪‹•›⟫

The month of Celi, the end of summer

After the dramatic events at the end of Tuvath, I was glad to have a breather to think. Tages had seen the wisdom of changing his ways. I'd not witnessed any confrontation or reconciliation between husband and wife, and was glad. We had work to do and had to travel to do so, generally in areas of harvest.

The end of summer is a time to reap the last harvest of summer's bounty, and if one has seed, plant the fall crops, which are rarely as abundant as summer's wealth. Men would be preparing to hunt, and not just training young hunters fresh from their initiation wounds, but real hunting.

Kutu had explained, since most of the hunting myths were kept by men, that men hunted all the time for food. While still true, grain farming had changed some things. He knew that in places of cultivated fields, an autumn hunt was useful in ensuring that fully grown deer and antelope did not decimate fields in a night. In cattle lands, this was, of course, less of an issue. But this was when they would often look at which cattle they'd nurture through the winter, rather than slaughter. Slaughtering cattle and preserving meat in the upcoming months meant that herds would not starve in winter. Preserved field grasses and grains would keep the lucky ones alive. Looking at the harvest was, even in Thefarland, highly important in all these plans.

There are some foreign stories of the early harvest gods being female, with drawings and sculptures of maiden women carrying sheaves of grain in their arms. In southern Obrone, the harvest god was male. One did not have to be Cai—with his words in spring about plows tilling into the earth—to imagine the violence of long blades cutting down the grain. The month of the Obrone's end of summer was named after a God of Earth—not of earth that feeds the seeds, which is feminine, but of earth's bounty being hacked from its mother seeds.

Celi is another month where young boys are removed from their mothers, in ceremonies often as violent as harvesting grain. I almost preferred the rituals of the Hunting Cults. Farmer tools for harvest are not passive.

As Tages wanted me safe in the Westvell, he didn't see why we shouldn't travel together.

Having been raised in remote scrub and woodlands, and the last several months in predominantly cattle country, I had not seen the damage harvest tools could do. We were needed, and saved a lot of limbs and fingers and toes.

Tages and I traveled together to Ravantha's manor, and took many side stops into her villages so that he could see what I had seen: the subtle illness sickening the land and the villagers on either side of the border. Less and less subtle now.

For Tages, it seemed to have the added merit of giving

himself distance from Velia. I was less certain that his wife needed even *less* attention than before. But he was still my master. I knew that he was finally doing his proper work. It was a necessary trip for a number of good reasons.

In this season, we often bound up the blisters on hands unused to the steady rhythm of swinging the blade from a scythe's long handle. Household pantries could heal most of these expected wounds, but there were sometimes far more serious injuries. We witnessed both the power and sharpness of the scythe. Tages and I cleaned and sewed up those wounds, and were often glad of four hands.

"Thank all the gods for science," he said to me in Ndeb, after one long surgery. "In years past, they would lose their legs, feet, or hands."

I nodded. I'd read almost as much as he had. I replied, "Clean surgical tools being one of the best revelations of science."

I thought of the divine white clay and the need for cleanliness in much of our work. With my new, rather petulant eyes, without purification, the clay was just dirt, no matter the color.

"Sickle and scythe are indeed weapons of great note," Tages said to me, after I'd commented on one particularly bad wound. Our patient had passed out even before I could dose him. Tages cleaned the wound, but had me, with my more delicate touch, sew all the bits back together. It was a long cut, rather than a stab, so he had chosen not to cauterize it.

Instead of going through the woods, staying at Grandmother Turani's house, or the ancient temple, we walked along the various byways. It was slow progress, turning back to the main road often to visit yet another village.

Tages chose to do this so he could reconnect with all the villages he'd neglected, and a few that I had not been able to visit. Venturing out early in the morning, we'd see places where mothers had left bowls by the side of the road.

Wherever the boys were being initiated was at least half a day away from those bowls. These rituals were ancient and a bit more brutal than the symbolism of the leaving of a daughter from a mother. It was something women were not to see, just as men did not see women's rituals.

We came near one place with bowls in an early evening. Tages had us walk back down the road a bit and move into a shaded underbrush and wait. I soon realized he wanted to hold back so that the women coming slowly down the road would not be disturbed by our passing. "We can sleep in the woods," he'd said. We were far enough back where they would not notice us unless they looked.

One by one, each woman bent down to pick up her bowl, now empty. The fourth woman wailed. Her son's bowl had not come back.

"Damn," said Tages, looking into the distance, where the boys and men might be.

I knew this woman's son would not be coming home, neither as a man nor to remain a child. He had not survived the ritual. Like a scythe cutting grain with graceful violence, the month of Celi also cut boys into men. Some survived.

I yearned to go and comfort the woman in the embrace of her friends.

"Is there anything we can do?" I asked, as if the men would have accepted my aid. They might have with my adept scar.

"It is too late," he said.

Tages turned to me, his face grim. "It is a terrible thing to say, as a Doctor-Diviner bemoaning the end of his profession's dignity quite clearly in view, but there are some ancient ways I wish would speed along with me to die out, never to return!"

I sighed and did not hide my tears, seeing his fall as well. "Some traditions die out too slowly."

We waited for darker night before we went down the road. Before we stood, I asked, "Does Kutu do this kind of thing? Circumcision, right?"

Tages shook his head, but said, "Of course. He knows, however, how to keep his knives both sharp and clean. More, he knows times are changing. He is beginning to hunt differently now."

Our journey was not only to care for blisters or mourn another lost boy.

Tages was finally making his own assessment about the state of the surrounding landscape. He could see the tension in the towns and shook his head at not having done anything about it.

He was glad now, doubly so, that he had decided to ensure my safety by traveling through the Westvell with me. He had not understood the pressures I was under—nor the extent of what I had witnessed. I did point out that it was not only Thefare or Fuluns who I feared. On our long walk to Ravantha's manor, I'd hoped to discuss many things with Tages, including my suspicions about Marce's state of health and ask what it might be. Instead, Ravantha and her situation dominated our discussion. Our discussions didn't seem to include the distant Aranthur, or his son Marce, as much as his desire for Thielle's broken necklace had been the original spark for all this growing tension. I still felt as if this should matter.

"It occurs to me," said Tages, "That Ravantha's thoughts are truly neither focused on you or your future. Her pain is all of the past. Your going to her for protection will not help either her or Thefare... or Fuluns." After a moment's thought, he added, "or even Aranthur. They are all wounded by the rape, for different reasons. You may have divined a battle, but think of something Thefare said," he suggested.

"What was that?"

"Do you remember he blamed Ravantha's blood for ruining negotiations?"

"Yes."

"How much did he want the Westvell?" he asked. "Why was it so important to him that he'd consider giving up a priceless necklace for it?"

I thought of the vision I had last spring. "Pride. Richer, more landed men than he came begging for this tarnished, broken thing. It had little value to him, except as a piece of history. It wasn't even, to him, the relic Aranthur is hoping it is. It was some proof of his lineage's former power and his own, what with all that tempting attention."

"Yes. I think he dickered over the price—mainly for show, as he saw no real value in Thielle's necklace other than that it had been in his family's coffers for generations—he would have been grateful to gain that land for something he did not quite realize was beyond price. He needed it, even as he's obviously trying to make a move to not require it. Foolishly, I might add, from what I have seen."

"How so?" I asked, glad to feel like a student again.

"The Westvell has income beyond cattle. It would have increased his wealth. Without it, he will have to slaughter too many cattle to turn over their grazing land into some kind of wheat —I think he's considering spelt, from what I could see of what was left of Pesne's burnt seeds. But he'll have to buy modern plows and hire men who know what they're doing to till and sow the land with grain. If he doesn't hire at least an experienced overseer, he'll waste the effort. Even so, he could not recoup his losses from all that expenditure as quickly as those who had long lost their herds and began growing grain before modern inventions of plows and threshing machines. The wealth he wants will take time."

I laughed ruefully. "So, in some ways it's *your* fault for healing his herds!"

"For the cattle side of things. He ought to blame his brother for the other!"

"I noticed he blamed Ravantha for being raped, rather than his brother for raping her," I said.

"She had gone willingly into the room," Tages said.

I had almost said something like that to her. I should have told her something akin to what I now told Tages.

"You're blaming the *victim*? She did not know he'd sent the guards away. She went with him, trusting. She also did not know her father had rejected Fuluns's suit for her hand, and so, had no idea that he had revenge in mind. She did not offer herself. He tricked her and took her by force. Unless you think her head wound part of consensual sex?"

Tages nodded. "You are right. I am ashamed, but so it is for many men, to blame the woman for temptation."

"That's disgusting," I said.

"I know. She could not have known that Thefare sent him away because he was a selfish and brutal thug who had done such things before. That rape of her was a final straw."

"Was it? When he was greeted with such fanfare by his brother? Thefare should have exiled him, like Velia's grandmother would have done."

I thought of the last moments at the house, with a tight-lipped Velia who was paying for her husband's neglect in far too many ways. We'd left her to pick up the pieces of her own mistaken trust. Fuluns was still riding that triumph fairly high.

An insight inspired a tight-lipped grin. "Which is why you gave Velia that huge pot of the consound salve I'd made before we left? Did you divine the need for that, or did you know it would be useful?"

"For the friendship she'd had with Arntlei, and how she used it—she will have much to redeem. Without knowing it, she has stuck a thorn in Fuluns's side, and Thefare's, because of her misguided negotiations. Arntlei will pay for it. The consound will heal her bruises, and possibly a few other unfortunate women in his path."

"Consound will hardly salve worse wounds, but Velia is adept in that kind of Medicine," I said, knowing she'd cope.

At least I knew he'd not abandoned her merely to walk with me to Ravantha's manor. But what terrible reasons to require her skill.

"Larce told me Fuluns had forced another woman who eventually killed herself. Thefare seems not to mind that sort of consequence for rude privilege. What about Hastia? Will she be safe?"

"She is too valuable, even without you as part of the marriage contract. I have reason to believe that Pesne can offer a great deal of grain seed with his bride price. Hastia might still marry the man she expects to marry."

I shook my head. "This is depressing."

"Marriage?"

"He is leveraging a girl's life for the regret in asking you to keep his cattle healthy, and his disapproval about a girl who trusted the wrong man who ruined yet more plans," I said.

"And to your mind, Ravantha has done the same."

"You don't think so?" He did not reply, so I added, "Believe me at least that she will not heal till *she* chooses to do so, whatever else you attempt. She has great pride in her anger, and the strength it seems to give her—all proud armor. Neither you nor I can help her till she does."

Mother or not, I was growing quite proud of that armor.

We said nothing for a while, and walked on for a few more paces. However much my pride might grow, there was a reality we were witnessing that had reverberating consequences.

"The long-term consequences of her head injury," I said, "have probably also given her problems of more fire and faulty logic. Not all her actions seem rational."

He nodded and then waved his hand. "Don't forget that this land was ready for her justified loathing toward him. Many of these people starved while Thefare's people ate beef and cheese. The people along the border—as you observed—were already ripe for growing distrust for their neighbors."

"A few still speak; I saw some proof of amicable trade that neither side acknowledged."

When her manor house was in view, Tages reminded me, "You cannot speak to her about Fuluns, or what happened at Hastia's fete. It will only fuel Ravantha's rage."

"I doubt it will matter. If I'm not mistaken, that is Larce's horse. He probably already shared everything he knows."

I'd forgotten that Larce had left Thefarland the day after that disastrous celebration, and no doubt made better time than we had. When we arrived, it became clear that she did not need our words to fuel any anger. He had indeed told Ravantha all he knew or guessed. He'd told Ravantha what Thefare had done, and learned that Pesne and Thefare may very well have seen her supposed daughter almost unclothed.

I had not thought to see Tages become even more grim than he had before hearing about details I had purposely left out. He aged before my eyes, becoming burdened by the weight of it all. I could say and do nothing. It was his cost for putting his head too far into the books we both loved.

He left before his own irritations with his distraction could betray him.

I also knew that he left quickly because he wanted no tales to be told to Thefare. He indicated to me that he had seen quite enough to confirm some of what he'd seen in his divination and all I'd written that had come too late to his notice.

Larce said something to him before they parted ways at the bottom of the steps, one to return to Thefarland, the other to the nearby village. Even before those words, Tages's posture, as he walked away was as grim as I'd ever seen him.

Soon after he left, I discovered that Ravantha was also leaving. I knew she traveled her land when I was not in residence, but I could not hide how perplexing this was, even as welcome a change as it was.

"I must go see my people," she said, coming out, arrayed in intricately embroidered finery. I realized that she'd planned this long before Tages and I had arrived. It was clear her preparations by then had been well underway.

With a thin-lipped smile that was too grim for any sort of cheer, she added, "When I have seen my people, I am going to treat with Thefare," she had said, "for having the audacity to make plans for my daughter."

If I thought Velia and her friends understood fashion and finery, I realized I was mistaken. I had never seen Ravantha dress for a fete, though I now learned she had enough finery in her wardrobe and clothes press to meet that kind of social challenge. She pulled out all the stops.

She went arrayed in finery, her hair curled and adorned as if for a wedding feast, but wearing her somewhat mannish clothing, which was yet made with all the modern notes to high fashion. She went and stood in a high-wheeled chariot that was gilded and decorated with apotropaic gods to frighten away harm. Women arrayed in splendor—and some men—mounted horses to ride alongside her.

There was a carriage that I'd watched be filled with clothes and decorations and a couple of servants to dress her. Clearly, she had packed even more so that she could be fresh and beautiful at each village she visited. If she did go all the way to Thefare's castle, no doubt she'd be fully armed upon arrival.

"What if I ask you not to treat with Thefare?" I asked.

"I am going, Sen. He has insulted us too many times!"

"But this..." I pointed at the weapons in her chariot. "You cannot do this. Fight him?" In this day and age, a civil war in Obrone was unheard of. There were means to settle disputes that had little to do with fighting. That incurred ostracism, as she no doubt knew. Perhaps she was used to this. Marce and Larce's visit surely didn't mean she met with any of the lords and ladies nearby. Her father, Rasce, wasn't even allowed to set foot in her lands.

I tried a ploy that was so manipulative that I trembled in shame.

"You're leaving me?" I asked.

"I must, my little one. I'm going to fight him if he will not respect me or my child!" She looked around her. "My people have long hated his land."

I knew this was not true.

"But you know nothing of war, of battle," I said.

She bent down and said, low, angry, "I have trained all your life for this moment."

I could only hope that her rage would diminish as it often did. The chariot was no less bouncy than a horse. She would soon be in pain.

"Can you not take the carriage?" I asked, believing it wouldn't help unless it was better sprung than a chariot. It might be better than riding a horse.

"No! I wish my people to see me, and so that Thefare can see me coming and see I am not diminished by his behavior!"

It was clear to me that her intentions were fixed.

"Take this," I said, rummaging in my bag, "for your trip. You will need it."

She looked at me, as if I had given her a precious gift, although the bundle I gave her was a bag full of the herbs that would diminish the headache she would no doubt get, as well as plenty of balm to—hopefully—diminish any irrational rage spurring on the rational.

The provocation was real. I could not deny that. I had seen the signs that something like this might happen, and Tages had confirmed it with—I had to admit—divination and observation that had come too late. Still, this display of wealth, beauty, and strength seemed as gaudy and awful as using an embroidered Westvellian ribbon to bind a suppurating wound. There was a triumphant gleam in her eye that made it stranger and more terrible.

I did not like the look Marce and Larce exchanged as her procession moved out. I knew that they disliked being apart for long, and yet they were parting ways again. It might not have caught my notice, except for that look Ravantha did not see. It was as determined as she had been exultant. I wondered if they now had as many reservations about all this as I'd had for too long. Did they now regret what they had made?

Chapter Thirteen

While Marce went with Ravantha, Larce stayed behind to act as a nominal guard, or jailor, for me. Nominal, because she had set women guards for the manor house, and Larce was still not allowed to stay overnight. I was guarded more than if Ravantha had stayed.

I spent the next couple of days training with Larce, though his lessons were uninspired. He seemed concerned about Marce or some unrevealed trouble. I found myself leaving his sour company as soon as I could. I mostly read what books Tages had left with me, and cataloged the pile of herbs I'd brought with me to study. When I was not doing any of those things, I spent most of my time in the kitchen with Mena and Ziia. I'd met them last spring during a memorable stay.

These things palled quickly, however. I was used to doing far more, I realized, than a few hours of training and reading. While I could no longer envy Tages's absorption in his studies, I didn't have enough of my own and knew I had to pace myself.

Adept

Early on, it became clear that the nights were a bit more entertaining, at least for the women guarding the manor.

Cafatia, the head guardswoman, informed me of this during one of our sparring sessions. Larce had already left in a huff, and Cafatia had taken over. He apparently was still irked by having been stopped from entering areas of the house which once, apparently, had been open to him. The guards prevented him from exploring alone, even if he said he'd only wanted a bath. I hadn't complained about the change in instruction. It was good to spar with a woman.

"Lady Ravantha was right to set guards. Someone has tried each night to enter this manor," she said.

"Oh!"

"Yes. Clearly, it is a good thing you are to be guarded well. We will increase the security."

"How much more secure do you need this place to be?" Already, no man was allowed in without an escort.

"Our mistress is not here. I will not betray her trust when that which she values over all things is under our protection and care," Cafatia said.

After a few days of sparring, study, interspersed with boredom, I had to admit to myself that I was more disturbed by past events. Cafatia and I were sparring at the flat space at the top of the stairs in front of the manor house. Larce lurked below.

I watched his movements during some necessary breaks. In my distraction, I had not noticed that Larce was favoring an arm. Tages would deplore my observational skills, even after I'd proved them so well scant days before!

When we were done with practice, I made my way down to confront him.

"Why are you favoring your right arm? I cannot believe you've trained me so well that you must use your left to spar with me."

He shook his head. "It has been seen to."

"You are talking to a Doctor-Diviner. If it had been seen to, you'd not have to favor it like that."

"You're an adept," he said pointedly.

"True, but you are still favoring your arm. I'm not so good with this staff as you'd like me to be, but I am good enough at my art to help you. What is wrong?" I said, moving forward, touching his arm and eliciting a sharp gasp of pain.

With reluctance, he let me examine his arm. He had to take off his shirt, to the annoyance of Cafatia. It was so injured that even rolling up his sleeve put too much pressure on it.

I shook my head. "The fire at Thefare's castle: That's when you were injured?" I asked.

He nodded.

"This is not healing well," I said. "If you do not let me help heal this, the wound will fester. If it festers, you will lose muscle mass, if not the arm. Let me help you."

Cafatia would not let him pass into the manor, on the off chance my work would end up having him stay the night. "It is too close to dusk," she said.

"Cafatia, he's injured. You can no doubt overpower him," I said.

She snorted. "That's a given." She was a rather burly woman, so it was probably not an egotistical statement, but the bare truth. Especially as Larce, lean strength that he had, was far more weakened by his arm than he'd let on. She would not budge, not even to let my patient rest nearby under supervision.

"No, I will not let him stay," she said. "Besides, he's gone on well enough without your care so far. To the village he goes!"

I followed with my healer bag. After ordering other women to take her post, she followed as well.

It took time to clean his wound of old skin. It was clear that the original burn had blistered and badly. It was delicate work, for the wound was not healing well. Someone had tried. I groaned.

"Who did this to you?"

"Ravantha. Interfering woman! She patched me up and put me to bed. Then she even sorted out all my travel gear and cleaned my underthings."

"She did not!"

He grinned, but winced in pain as I worked. I was being as careful as I could, and even then, I could not help but hurt him. "True. She had a servant do that. She really ought to have a doctor here, if not some herbal woman, or keep you here. But she treated the wound. She even went so far as to let me stay the night—guarded by Cafatia, her new protégé—and cleaned up all my travel gear. She said she'd watched you tend a servant girl."

"Yes. Weeks ago. Clearly, she didn't hear that I needed to let part of the girl's burn not be salved, so the heat from the wound would not be trapped. This is a pus-filled mess."

The servant boy for his rooms in the village would not give me his name, nor would any of the people in the house—all too cowed or horrified possibly to have Ravantha's *daughter* tending a man in his own rooms! I gave orders for them to make an infusion of herbs, and gave him pellets Tages had finally made up using all the equipment in my hut.

"These will help boost your healing from the inside. At least you no longer have a burn."

"I can't believe I can't stay at the manor."

"You've never stayed at the manor, have you?"

"Only when she tended my burns. But Ravantha is not in residence, and she wants me to protect you. How can I do that a quarter mile away?"

"You'd hear them coming?"

He snorted, and I continued to carefully clean the wound.

"But, Sen," he said, "I could... I would like to spend more time with you, but that Cafatia! She won't let me. As if I would importune your honor!"

There was a tone in his voice I was only familiar with in Cai's teasing. "Excuse me?" I said, looking up.

"You are a lady and lord's daughter."

"There is *no* proof of that," I said. "And what point would there be if there were?"

"We could marry."

I could not help it. I snorted in derision. It wasn't that he was too old for me, though there was a gap, but for some reason, I didn't think marriage was something he'd choose.

"With what dowry?" I asked—but then suddenly thought of my part of Thielle's necklace, and all the other jewelry and coins I'd found in Grandmother Turani's coffers. They were not rich pieces, by any means; they would not be wealth equal to Larce's prospects, even had I any interest in him at all.

"You are Tages's servant," he said. "And if we married, I could spend the night with you in that lonely hall."

I was not lonely in that hall, spending a good portion of my time enjoying the company in the kitchen, and relieved to have peace and quiet of the house, and no one watching me bathe or sleep, ready to go into a rage because she thought I was unhappy about the temperature of my soup.

I shook my head.

"For one, Larce, I'm not a servant. I'm an adept. I've studied long enough that I can ensure your wound heals. Regardless of Ravantha's wishes, I am bound to my mentor. I cannot marry till I am a master of my craft." I thought of Gavius, and thought, *I wouldn't pick you, Larce*. Then I focused on picking out some dirt that had been embedded in the original wound. "Then I can do as I wish."

I could not help but think his wishes to woo me were odd at best. I finished my work quickly and walked back under Cafatia's escort. I was glad of her presence. I was too deep in thought that I'd have gotten lost.

Why was Larce suddenly interested in marrying me—when he'd shown no interest at all? Aule, who was the closest I had to a brother, had shown more interest than Larce ever had till this point. Heavens, Professor Cuintus—who had never met me— showed more real interest, though not of a romantic nature. There was no point in speculating more. I could not answer my questions.

The next few days, I took the time to finish cataloging the last of my gathered herbs and transliterating what I knew as they were known in Ndeb. I'd sent a copy to Aule to show Professor Cuintus, and see if it was something I could work into a paper worthy of publication. After that, boredom truly set in—something that became increasingly aggravating as the days turned to weeks.

When I asked Larce what was taking Ravantha so long, he only stated that she was traveling to other parts of her land.

He continued his odd pursuit of my hand, so I quickly ended the conversation, as his wooing of me became far too disconcerting. I focused on tending his arm, which was healing quite well finally.

Keeping my distance, I trained with Cafatia instead, stating that Larce needed to heal, which was true. If she noticed I was avoiding my friend, she said nothing. If anything, she felt pride in being my teacher over a man. She was always ready to dismiss men. She groused that even Ravantha's beloved Marce exemplified the fickleness of men.

She gave me a long list of his behaviors I'd not seen, which I let wash over me to avoid the gossip, as I focused on defending myself from her easy attacks on me. She would prattle the whole session, even as I struggled to block her blows or aim my own. I could not help but store some interesting information about Marce's illness, filed away into the pocket of my mind, which I had yet to discover or research.

Marce could often get irritable, rising from a difficulty in organizing his thoughts. He'd had emotional outbursts, which apparently Larce did his best to cover up. There were rumors that he'd had a seizure. I wondered about that, as I had myself seen some chorea in his movements.

With each session of training with her, the load of irritations grew.

Not wishing to feed that level of misandry, I began to avoid both martial teachers. Without enough to occupy me, I finally started exploring the manor. The other women only went through it to dust periodically, but most of it was not in use, except my room, the servant quarters, and the kitchen. I'd taken to dining in the servants' hall, which was far more pleasant than dining alone.

There was nothing much to see in that large, rambling house. Certainly, there were no lower region for servants to work or live in, unless by chance it was under some upper room. There was no basement on all that granite. The running water itself was a feat of engineering that defied any thoughts that ancient cultures were in any way primitive, since the house clearly rested on the bones of something older. It was larger than Tages's house, and smaller than Thefare's castle. I could see Ravantha had more wealth than Thefare, though. Everything that filled her home was of good quality. I even explored the attics, but found little to occupy me.

The last room I explored was her bedroom.

I'd gone in there as little as possible, but had that one other occasion seen the quality of her clothes, many of which had gone with her. This time, I looked over what was left of her personal armory. A person could use at most two swords at a time. Six were left on display.

The only thing that interested me was a small knife that was sharp enough for me to consider for surgery. It was sharp enough for postmortem dissection as well. It might allow me to make small, clean cuts to lift out organs for examination without damage. I sat on her bed, as it was nearby, and tested it with my finger and then the end of my leather belt.

Sitting down on her bed, I shifted the bedding and her pillows. I got up and smoothed the cover absently and fluffed the pillows as best I could. A blue ribbon gleamed from under a pillow, lit by a gleam of amber sunlight. I pulled at it. It was tied or stuck to something. I followed it with my fingers and found it tied to some kind of nail or protrusion. I pulled on the other end of the ribbon. It had weight to it.

Without even seeing what it was, I began to tremble. My hands were shaking so badly, my fingers could barely open the soft, embroidered bag.

It was Thielle's necklace from my vision, minus the small amber and a few beads—presumably sewn onto her daughter's first clothes—and the piece in my own bag.

A surge of disgust, like bile, rose in me. No wonder she'd looked triumphant. Had she really gone to start a war? Or was this whole gilded procession a way to shove her triumph in Thefare's face?

No wonder Larce was peevish. His knowledge of the Amantile tea, the fire, his hasty departure. Granted, his sickened wound wouldn't cheer a well-fed duck. She had, in that ghastly display, claimed his feat, his theft, really—so perhaps some of his feelings ought to be relief? And then another thought entered my head: how often someone had tried to get in. Cafatia thought it was to get to me, but this part of Thielle's necklace ought not be here. Logic quickly told me who had taken it—Larce's burned arm, the guardroom fire, drunken bets with the guard—he knew this was here. If he'd given it to her, why would he try to get it back?

Injured arm... Ravantha going through his things....

He had not given it to her. Was this why he was trying to get into the castle, claiming a sudden and surprising affection for me? It made far more sense that it was just a ruse to get the bauble back.

But why?

This damned necklace had been trouble from the beginning of its creation. It had inspired a god's defection from his intended bride, if the legends were true. That same god had chosen to give it to a goddess who had no reason to hope, who had become a champion of the hopeless. I thought of Grandmother Turani's objections to myths told around the fire.

Regardless, I suddenly felt certain that the necklace did not belong in Ravantha's treasury, much less Thefare's. It belonged in a temple, as whole as I could make it. Beyond the legend, it had clearly become the source of great pain for Ravantha and Thefare alike, as well as those who were related to them by blood or circumstance.

If it had never been in Thefare's possession, none of the growing tension would have risen. It was like a splinter stuck in a wound that sickened an entire arm.

I stood and took the bag with the necklace inside. I went straight to my chamber and put it in my shoulder bag. An idea had come into my head, and I did not know what to do with that thought. I felt at odds with my intention. I went in search of Larce, who was outside, near the base of the stairs, tending his white horse.

"Ah, there you are," Larce said. "You haven't had the chance to ride Achivizer in a while, and he's beyond our reach to saddle him for you. Perhaps you'd like to ride Moonlight?"

"No, I don't feel up to a ride. I'd like to take a walk, however," I said, seeing people around. "Will you join me?"

"Assuredly. I'm here to protect you."

I shook my head. "I don't think that there is anyone here who is really after me, but fine. Protect me all you want."

When I knew we were more or less alone and out of earshot, I asked, "Why weren't you allowed to go with Ravantha? Why aren't you back with Marce? He did not stay with her."

"How do you know that?" he asked.

"Something that Cafatia said. She was complaining about the fickleness of men, Marce especially."

"He's had to go speak with his father about a few things.

He's been gone too long. Do not worry, his father will send him right back."

"Send him?" I asked.

"Well, set him free? Don't worry, he's not left Ravantha. And as you can see, I'm here to hold the fort."

"This is not a fort."

"It will be, in a manner of speaking."

"So there really will be a battle?" I asked, appalled.

"There very well may be!"

"None of you has ever been trained for battle. You are far too young to have been part of the war with Dedathon."

I'd only seen a look as mulish on Ravantha. I was far younger than they, but I suddenly felt as if Ravantha was not the only unruly, irrational person in my care, but Marce and Larce were as well.

"If I can guess, you did not go because you cannot return to Thefare's?"

He turned away. "No."

"Why not? Tell the truth, or I will divine the truth from your lies, and it will go badly for you."

"What would you do to me?" he asked, condescendingly.

"Tell those who it would matter to," I said. I paused, wondering if I ought to reveal what I knew. "Do you not know that the Doctor-Diviner's art includes revealing what is secret when it sickens a community?"

He shook his head. "The Doctor-Diviners near my home are fools, which is why we go to a hospital or call a physician when we can, or even an apothecary for the servants."

"Talk to me."

"Well, over the past few months, if it brings you any

comfort, I see that you are not a fool, nor Tages. Fine, say what you think is so secret!"

"You stole something."

His eyebrows rose. "Indeed, I should not compare you and your master against the idiots I've met before. I told Tages, before he left, to watch over Velia. It is possible she will be blamed."

"For what?"

"The potion I gave the treasure guards. I drank with them, but not as much. They fell asleep. I did not. I stole that damned necklace Ravantha now has in her keeping. I wasn't going to show it to her. I was telling Marce! He's my cousin, and more! And it's everything to me! If I gave it to his father, I could have property and income. I wouldn't be the poor relation anymore. He could get away from family life, then, on our own property. Mine. Instead of coming here. I got here, in so much pain that I was fainting. She probably overheard me bragging to Marce, and when she tended me herself, claiming some skill from you, she found it and kept it."

He was clearly revealing more than I'd asked.

"And Thefare's guards didn't suspect you?"

"I'll admit I am surprised I got away with it! I'm not a thief at heart. I hid it, and then slept with them by the guard room. We were all supposedly given the same sleeping potion. A cursory glance showed that nothing much was missing. There was only fire damage from a fallen candle to that damned contract between Thefare and Pesne, and some grain seeds."

"I can't believe he actually kept those in the treasure room," I said.

Larce shrugged. "He *valued* them!" His tone was all derision.

I shook my head. "Well, you paid some cost with those

actions. You might have lost your arm! I must go see if Tages and Velia are safe! You risked *their* lives for that broken necklace. It's just a bauble!"

"No, it's not. It's something that could gain Marce his father's land now, and me some as well. Aranthur has been wanting it for longer than Marce has been alive, and his desire for it has grown even greater. He thinks owning relics and statues and crafting a great temple on his lands makes him closer to the gods somehow. Proof of his devotion. One day, he'll be gifted the healing he needs, that *Marce* needs, that I know he'll need. One day. Even a man like Thefare valued it as equal to all of the Westvell. He should have just given it to Rasce and taken the land—and Rasce the same! Defiled daughter or not."

I was shocked at his words. "You can't mean that!"

"Why not?"

"Ravantha is your friend."

"Yes, a friend who values that necklace and you equally. So, you cannot leave." He grimaced. "Cafatia will soon have guards looking for you to bring you back to that damned manor of Ravantha's. I didn't need to be here guarding you. I didn't stay for you, or for her. She has all those women guarding you even now. I am here to keep that *bauble* safe for Marce's sake, and mine—my injured arm my excuse. I plan on getting it back."

I looked up at him. He wanted to get the necklace for Marce and himself, and his uncle, Lord Aranthur, who had wanted it from the beginning. I schooled my face so I could not show any disgust. Aranthur had cared even less about Ravantha in all this than Fuluns, Thefare, Marce, or Larce. I flashed back to the memory of Hastia's celebration. All those painted faces, no personality behind them. Objects for the proud men to move and use. As if all that paint still itched my skin, I could see how we were being moved about by others.

I rubbed my face as if to remove the paint again.

"It is just an old, broken necklace," I said, knowing it was not.

"I know what you're thinking, but Aranthur has given over much of his ruling to study alchemy. This thing was made by the gods, and it heals. It transforms an awful thing into something good. Ugliness to hope. He needs it. Aranthur..." he paused. "*Marce* needs it," he said, with strange emphasis on his friend's name.

I examined Larce's eyes and face for any other revealing expressions. I wondered if he realized that he'd shared more than I had seen or guessed. Aranthur had wanted it for his own reasons, enough to coerce Rasce to give away his daughter's considerable estate for it. Thefare had valued property over an ancient bauble—and rightly so, as the bauble wouldn't feed his people, or the people he would rule over. I could not think too kindly of Thefare, however; he'd had no problems adding me to the dower of his niece, as if I were just as much of a thing as Thielle's broken necklace.

It was strange to see how their assessed value of an object or girl proved how meanly they actually thought of them. At least to my eyes. The true value of the necklace was denied by all of them, proven by their false value of me. It did not matter to any of them that I'd been taken from my mother and exposed to the elements to die. It did not matter that for most of my life, till the age when I became an adept, they'd *never* bothered to inquire about me. I was an adult by age, regardless of the lack of any Milk Tree ceremony or Doctor-Diviner scars. They'd spent at least seventeen or eighteen years *not* bothering to wonder if Grandmother Turani's foundling was their lost daughter or niece.

It wasn't as if I was in hiding, working with Tages all these months. I'd played a significant part in many a ritual Medicine.

Thefare had made plans with Velia's assistance. Ravantha had not really made me part of her plans like a game piece till he'd done so, except to look at me as if I were some precious jewel. She'd used the probable insult to me to gather up her army before treating with Thefare—or rather, to boast her success and flaunt her obvious wealth in revenge.

With a shudder, I realized that it was still not at all about me—it was all about Thielle's necklace, which I now had both parts of, minus the bits that had been sewn into Ravantha's baby's gown. I felt tied to it somehow, with a kinship to it rising from how all these people had treated us.

"You all disgust me," I said, turning from Larce, and stalked back to the manor.

I gathered up my bag and supplies and told Cafatia that I believed that there was some sickness in a village nearby. I could smell it on the wind. She sent me off with one of her guardswomen, Ndellie—a surprising name that mixed old and new. As we walked away, I thought it interesting that Cafatia was there to guard the manor more than me. Or rather, what was supposedly in the manor.

I called upon Jackal for aid, feeling bad about the rage Ndellie might meet when it was all said and done. I had to get away and lick my wounds and think.

Ndellie was not prepared for a jackal pack. We were walking down the road, the wind in our face, and still she did not smell the jackals coming. One moment, the road was lonely, and even clear of man or beast. The next, jackals surrounded us with yips and yowls. We were separated as we ran from the pack. I, too, felt fear for most of that run, till I was cut off and they turned to Ndellie, and I wondered if I'd have to stop and patch her up. She pulled out her bow and let some arrows fly. None of them made their mark, and I realized that the pack was all Jackal. He laughingly tricked her and enjoyed our fear.

He set her running back to the manor house, no doubt to add to the alarm. I had an after-image of him nipping at her heels, even as he sat next to me and cackled.

Jackal and I turned onto his Way and walked toward Grandmother Turani's stone house.

When we were down the road a long way away, I thanked him.

"You will do well to learn more of this road, Sen of the Woods. Your time on the White Road, the White River, is nearly done."

"The White Road?" I asked, and suddenly the image of the white Mastery scar came to mind. "Do you mean I will no longer be a healer?"

"You will be—you must be, Sen!" And he laughed, his lips lifting in a near-snarl of laughter that made all his teeth exposed, red with blood. "You will be more."

He disappeared, with that last look of his making me shudder. I'd had enough of men or women deciding who I was or what my future would be. I realized that I was now bound to this teacher in a way I never had been with Tages—and I had no idea of the lesson.

For the first time, I remembered that he wasn't just clever and canny, a useful guide. He was a predator. I remembered

Ndellie's fear and his teeth red from a bite. He was Jackal and had always been.

He was not a safe creature to have aligned with! I was frightfully sorry I had called on him last spring.

Book of Autumn

Chapter Fourteen

The month of Letun, the birth of autumn

Letun was a Mother goddess, perhaps a harvest goddess. She had given birth to twins, like Tuvath. Much of her story was embedded in stories of other gods. I only understood her as being a rival to other Mother gods or Earth gods. She was a little less benign than the height of summer. For her, it was the twins, you see, that gave her month power— because twins were out of the natural order.

Why Tuvath was celebrated for twins, and Letun was not, I did not know. Perhaps because Tuvath could be forgiven with a child of great beauty, despite her ugly twin, where Letun's children were otherwise unremarkable.

Names of the goddesses with similar attributes made me wonder who the original gods of Obrone might have been, even for this reason, if they could be that specific. Did it matter? So many stories, so many gods traded and bandied about, their attributes and stories mingling and overlapping.

It gave me the heretical idea that there weren't any gods at all—at least not as we knew them—but that there might be archetypes who seeded stories all over the world, as varied as the people who told them.

Did that matter? One day it might not. The gods I knew might just be names on a calendar, with people forgetting all but snippets of who they are, their power dying like the profession of Doctor-Diviner.

People would forget that Letun had once had twins, and just know it as a word naming a month of often unaccountable weather.

It was a month that could herald shifts to nature that threatened the regular order of seasons, echoes of her unruly twins.

It was a month of late summers, when some canny gardeners or farmers could get yet another bounteous harvest in. Or not. Last year, Letun brought a brief, biting season of winter before returning to a more reasonable autumn—breaking a tree branch that wept into my hand.

In general, the start of autumn had always been my favorite time of year. Harvest was coming in, and babies conceived in the previous late autumn or early winter started to arrive. Velia rarely let me help her usher the babies into the world. However, the birth of babies was a community affair. Tages was often invited to the fetes to divine if the family's ancestors approved of the new member of the family. Everyone got to make a bit of a fuss over the babies, including me, who was often left to tend the baby while everyone else celebrated the parents' good tidings.

This year, I went not to a new life, but to my past.

After escaping Ravantha's manor, I went back to Turani's old house and stayed there as both a retreat and home. To my joy, there was a stack of empty journals, books, and slim dissertations waiting for me, left by Tages. And a note.

In Ndeb, Tages wrote that he hoped he'd predicted when I'd leave Ravantha's, and that there was a wealth of nature to explore. Being out and about seemed to renew his inner eye. He also indicated he believed that war would be slow in coming—neither Ravantha nor Thefare would ever destroy crop land or take people away from harvest. He wrote that all the land was surprised at Ravantha's gaudy display. He himself, despite his threshing basket, could not account for it. I was glad, though, that all she had done was shriek about her power.

While there was not a great deal of land that had been plowed in Thefarland, there was enough, and more in the Westvell. Crops gathered in early autumn prevented starvation in winter.

Tages had also left me herbs and some foodstuffs, including some beans, grains, and triangular dried pasta from one of his villages. He had also left one of Velia's cheeses. It was probably all the apology I'd ever get from the woman, but that gift of her bounty could be considered quite a considerable admission. I accepted it with pleasure.

I made myself a flat bread with one of Grandmother Turani's pans and ate it warm from the fire, with a gift of olives and that cheese, watching the dying day.

Before it went fully dark, I climbed up the worn, ancient steps that maidens of Thielle must once have used in their rituals. I left some of the bread and cheese there. As rough a teacher as he'd been, and disturbing, I did have something to thank Jackal for.

"I don't know what you want, Jackal, but I must give you

more gratitude for helping me leave the manor. I'm happy here." I set it down in his Way, and then left before seeing if it was still on the boulder, or if it would be eaten by birds or animals that roamed the night.

I'd forgotten how good the view was from there, so in the next days, I often took my meals up the rocks, and ate, and read.

I had no other duties except to study and roam the region. I felt as if I was given freedom by my mentor. I was safe, at least till as Ravantha discovered the necklace missing.

I explored late autumn glory, gleaning food from the harvest of nuts and berries, and the greens that abounded in cooler weather, adding to supplies that would no doubt dwindle. I only missed people. Not merely for their company, but because I wanted to help them. I had not realized how much my life had been motivated by Tages's influence, but also the joy of healing. Almost a full month without practicing my art helped me see how much it was my vocation, not merely because I'd been apprenticed to a Doctor-Diviner.

I remembered what Jackal said—that my time on the White Road, presumably studying the healing art, would soon be at an end. That there was more. That I would be more than a healer. I had no idea what that meant. It gave me pause, however. Was I done on the White Road or River, as he called it? At least he had said I would still be a healer.

It might not matter. I did not want to stay in an area filled with conflict—or rather, conflict that used me as a bargaining chip, or a necklace that belonged not to a man or a woman, but a goddess. Gods weren't bargaining tools for power or possession, either.

I'd have to be smarter than Jackal to get out of the trouble

I'd brought onto myself by stealing that necklace. Thefare and Ravantha would not care about my interpretation of a god's law or right of possession.

After a few days, I could not resist the pull or call I'd been sensing since the first night I'd slept in Grandmother Turani's home. I also went to visit Jammon's three-chimney ruins of a temple. The Tree, which had once blossomed in small white flowers, now had red fruit. I filled my bag with what it offered me. Some I stored at Turani's house. I was drawn to the place now, remembering more of Turani's song. I visited it often, sitting under the Tree, eating of its fruit, and contemplating what I could remember of the lyrics for the lullaby. I still only had eight lines, knowing there were more.

I visited it whenever I passed nearby, taking the time to sit and ponder its strange significance. Some of my reading was dissertations, among them the lore of spiritually significant trees in other cultures. I wondered how this Tree that only I could see might reflect or echo other stories.

Unlike those stories, this one was alive and entering the country's autumn. Watching as more of one side of the Tree began to die, I wondered what more must I learn? What was I to learn? I did not know. I could not look at the Tree that gifted me with fruit and be idle. I had to go out and do my work, and hopefully take the necessary steps to continue to learn.

Cai had been right, last spring, that one could not learn sitting in Tages's study. I had to apply it to learn more.

I began to go to villages nearby, rejecting all other accolades except being an adept to a Doctor-Diviner. I went to villages within a day's walking distance, or two days, if I could plan a place to hide. I danced for people's healing. I divined the truth of arguments and mediated the conflict. I somehow could always find a balance and a reason for each side, though divining the one thing—and possibly a few things—that bound the people in conflict was an art. I yearned to go back to Tages's home and learn more of this part of the Doctor-Diviner's art. I had too much science and not enough divination.

Without ancestors, that door still remained shut to me.

To hide from Thefare and Ravantha, I should not have gone to the villages in the Westvell. In one town, I learned that Ravantha was looking for me. She had been so bold as to name me her daughter, and the villagers called me Sen Ravanthine. They soon learned that if they did not correct that, I'd do healing, but no more. I'd disappear into Jackal's Way, where few could find me. I knew I could not hide like this for long. It was clear that Ravantha wanted to get a hold of me. I suspected it wasn't just to find me, but to find the part of the necklace she had thought to own.

Larce had, by some reports, also left. Maybe she'd believe he'd stolen it back?

I'd started using Jackal's Way far more often, especially when I had to lick the wound of a name that wasn't mine. I walked along a road carpeted with autumn leaves, a ground covered in red brighter than what had fallen.

In another village, a week later, I learned that Larce was on his white horse and looking for me as well. Not back to Aranthur's lands, then. If Ravantha had revealed that the necklace was gone, he was certainly bound by his loyalty to his friend and Lord Aranthur to find me as well, whatever he told her. It most likely rankled that I'd disappeared on his watch.

In the far reaches of Thefarland, I also heard that Thefare

was not pleased with his proud neighbor, who housed a thief. He was gathering up fighting men, those he could spare from either his meager harvest or guarding cattle. I felt bad for all the people who would be caught between them. Briefly, I thought about handing both of them half the necklace and letting them be done with it, but I also knew too well that their conflicts went beyond a god's bauble.

As I traveled, I ate what villagers gave me. The main source of my food, however, was fruit from a Tree no one else but I could see. The apple-like fruit was juicier, and yet somehow still meatier than an apple. Each time it tasted like blossoms, or sunlight, or a night breeze in branches. Each time it filled me with a sense of love.

In some ways, it was more and more my Milk Tree. Each day, I felt more at peace with a truth I no longer felt a need to fight for.

I could, most legitimately, say that my own inadvertent tree ceremony had made me an independent woman. It went beyond what I could claim as Tages's adept or future Master Doctor-Diviner. I was woman enough to make my own choices.

I went back to the ruined temple and sat under the Tree that had once crowned me with white flowers. Now apples might drop into my hand, and it always felt as if the branches were like arms, open and inviting me to sit with it a while. Crow was in its branches, like a dark blot among the red apples and green leaves. It cawed and then flew off to a tree nearby.

I sang the song Turani had sung to me, but I could only remember a fragment of the song. Sitting there, I realized that a daughter *had* been left here. If the lullaby was true. And then, like a rush, more came:

"One was wrapped
In lace and gold
Another leaves and dirt
One died in the cold
The other death did skirt

One was lost, another lives
Oh, the humble child
Into my arms did come
And though a gift to the wild
When held her heart did thrum

Cradled by this Tree's roots
One's destiny died at death
While her mother's tears did pour…"

As the words I remembered rolled around in my mind, I wondered if it meant that Grandmother Turani had lifted me from a ruined life of lace and gold—rather the gold color of amber and dying leaves—and brought me from dying in a blanket of dirt and leaves to live. When Grandmother Turani had taken me into her arms, had that made me *the humble child*? Did that song mean there were two babies, or that we were one and the same—like some myths implied about Thielle and Nhor—that they were one goddess with two aspects, harmony and warding off despair? I wondered if that was one reason she'd had me study with Tages. If I were exposed to die, how could she even begin to think the possible rich parents would want me back?

I shook my head. In no history that I had been told had *two* children been born to Ravantha.

I still could not believe I was Ravantha and Fuluns's child.

I sat trembling in the effort of rejecting that slim chance that I actually might be! Knowing I'd been exposed, that they had chosen to let me die, fueled the need to rebel against the thought. They were not my parents. What I remembered about the song described what might be my rich and humble beginnings.

Agitated, I stood to walk around the ruins. I turned to look at the Tree from the first vantage I remembered, when Cai and I had wandered here.

Despite the rot I could see from one side, it was a beautiful Tree that, when I looked at it in Jackal's Way, had apples that practically glowed in shades of vermilion. On the healthy side, it seemed as its bark twisted in a dance toward the sky, that it rejoiced in reaching to the heavens, even as I knew its roots went deep past the rock into the earth. I knew that there were places it broke through the rock, even as there were roots that embraced it.

Wind of the earth and wind from one of the Ways lifted branches in a dance that sang with the air's cool dance through the leaves.

I moved to look at and draw the tree from the dying side. It seemed almost as if the bark and branches were dropping or twisting down into the depths, below ground where something clearly gnawed at its roots—either rot or ants, or some other creature. The nearby Crow cackled at me from a dead branch. "There, there... follow when you can!" she said, laughing at my befuddled expression, then flew off to the north.

A gleam of light from the dusk's sun made something shine on the ground near the exposed rotting roots of the tree. It lay by some old, tumbled temple stone that was lifted by this ever-growing and ever-dying tree covered in a blanket of its old leaves. I froze for a moment. Then I went to investigate.

Under leaf litter and rock, I found the gleam of an amber pendant in tarnished silver.

I found more than that one small pendant. The roots, black with rot, had moved the earth, exposed some earth, and a bundle with stained white cloth, sewn with bits of blackened silver and still-bright amber gems. Small bones of a baby wrapped in fine lace and linen.

The newly remembered lines of the song thrummed in my mind.

"One was wrapped in lace and gold... Oh, the humble child," I said, my voice breaking.

I broke. A cry escaped me as I carefully gathered the swaddled bones wrapped in brittle lace into my arms and rocked the child that could have been. I wept onto the bones.

They'd made a glory of me, of who they wanted me to be.

All during these terrible weeks, they were building feelings of resentment and revenge that warmed their stone hearts. Not weeks, nor months, but *years* this child lay here forgotten by them all—even me!—remembered only in Grandmother Turani's lullaby, and all that song's meaning faded like many of the legends of the gods.

Some things ought not be forgotten or lost.

"You were here all along," I said.

I still did not remember the final words of the lullaby. It didn't matter. I knew enough. I knew that we had been found together by the only person who truly cared for me. Two babies, lying together, as if sisters, as if twins. The cold had taken the one in swaddling clothes, but Turani had taken me, the one wrapped in nature, into her arms. The one left in leaf litter and dirt. The humble child had survived.

I had proof. I was not Ravantha's daughter.

I was on my knees, weeping as I touched the tiny bones. Grief and guilt that I—less swaddled and warm—had somehow survived rose in me. I knew that Grandmother Turani had not come soon enough to save us both. And that I really had no known family. The twisted disgust of being Ravantha's daughter impaled the small, dead hope of having something, someone.

"How long did I lie with you?" I asked the bones. "Did we hold each other? Did I know when your body cooled? How could I not keep you alive, my sister?"

I wish I could have held this child a little longer, that maybe my warmth could have kept her safe long enough for Turani to come and gather both of us up. In some ways, she and Turani were my only family.

I set the bundle back down, careful of the skull, the only thing not protected by the swaddling gown. I took off my tebenna and covered her better. Wrapping the bundle with the long scarf, I could protect the whole. Without having any better idea of what to do, I put her in the bag with the broken necklace.

I wanted to give them both to Nhor, the ugly Goddess of Hope, the apotropaic god who would scare away all wickedness or danger. If she'd died in fear, could Nhor go back in time to help her feel safe?

I wanted to take this child who had been abandoned into the arms of a goddess who would protect her from the evil of neglect. I also wanted to take the necklace to the goddess who could understand how damaged and ugly a necklace could be used so badly.

I walked back to Turani's house and made a better swaddling for the baby's bones. I started to wrap the necklace with her, but I had another thought. I pulled out the fragment of jewelry Grandmother Turani had kept safe in her house. I laid the two pieces together. Turani's third almost made the necklace whole. With a shudder, I realized I had all the pieces of the necklace, except one amber gem. Crow cackled in the branches of a tree nearby, apparently returned on her swift and silent wings. With ostentatious gestures, she played with an amber gem.

Did that mean anything, except that it tied us all together?

I was well aware that my reasoning was not completely sound—but it was still, to my mind, far better than Ravantha's irrational thoughts, Thefare's greed, or Aranthur's various manipulations. If any of them were going to have it out, they could do it on their own terms and not use any of us to do so!

I finished wrapping the pieces of the whole necklace. I found fluff, cotton, and some rags, and put the child in a well-padded, protected bundle. I would not risk giving her more injury than she'd suffered. I filled another bag with the apples and other foodstuffs. I'd been gone an entire month. Disturbed that I had more to learn from Jackal, I was more than troubled by this.

I found no peace in the proof I was not Fuluns and Ravantha's daughter. In fact, that was almost more awful. It was like the paint on my face at Hastia's party, and the gilding of Ravantha's triumph. It was much darker and more bleak.

I started on my way back to Tages's house. I desperately needed to consult with my master.

Chapter Fifteen

⫷⫸

The Month of Hehunn, the Autumn Hunting Season

Hehunn is the season where hunting—and war—could begin, apparently without incurring the disgust of one's less tempestuous neighbors. At least if most of the harvest was in. Hehunn was Thielle and Nhor's father. Strangely, there were few stories that declared what he had done when Jammon caused such a muddle between the two sisters. He was known to provide for his family and was often the archetype of the perfect man.

Of all the gods, his stories were more like the tales Kutu told, of animals and their prowess. They were to illustrate and guide hunters, young and old, in their tasks. There were some that Kutu claimed were more modern.

He'd once said, "You can tell because they feature cattle. Of Hehunn outwitting even wily Jackal as he protects his herds, or making a rug of him to put at his feet while he feasts—a thing to prove his mastery over Jackal, to say it is an insignificant beast, a pest."

The older stories were, apparently, different. Some included animals tricking Hehunn, such as Jackal tricking him away from a herd of deer, or stories that hinted at and displayed how Rabbit hides. Kutu never told me all the stories in full. I'd only heard bits and pieces, as I was no hunter. Those were for the men of his cult.

Stories told at fetes during the hunting month—and whatever season was good for hunting any particular beast throughout the year—were of the hunters' prowess in bringing home game. From what I had heard, they were often less about that than how some *hunter* had protected the herd of cattle in their keeping.

"In the older stories," Kutu once told me, "they never have cattle. It is all about the hunt, how Hehunn teaches a respect for all the beasts he hunts, and those who might hunt him in turn. They are the stories told by my fathers for many generations."

"Your family has long been hunters?" I asked.

"We have long been leaders of the hunt. Now my family guards cattle or challenges those nobles on the hill to play as a sport. They test their use of a bow, or those new, noisy matchlocks. They know nothing of the game we hunt. For them, it's only meat on the table or a fierce creature they can best. All a weak measure for their pride.

He was not a nobleman, though his family's women were rich in their own right—and he, in the eyes of modern men, was as wealthy, even if he did not dress the part. He embodied the prowess of the god of his cult.

I remembered how Ravantha had had Marce and Larce go after a lion worrying a farming village. They had gone with a will, dressed in special clothes that looked a mere dull version of their more formal fashion, and with boots that rose up their calves. Even though she'd sent them off to join the men of the village, she'd shaken her head.

"They only go out for sport in their townships. At least they know how to listen to their factors. Where they live, they must hunt deer in season, as they have cultivated the land away from the lions and jackals and other predators. There are few natural predators, except humans, to eat the deer that can plow down a field in a night if there are too many."

"Well, they at least would then feed the village," I'd said, naive.

"Venison is for the table of the big house," she said, correcting me. "Perhaps we might share with the poor. I can already see that I must manage better. One day, the Westvell will be all cultivated. The meat will not be from the woods, but what cattle or fowl we have butchered and sold. At least we will not be like Thefarland, with their great bloody slaughter, thinning out the herds in preparation for winter."

In walking along the byways of the road, I was cautious. I reflected that while nature had once limited deer and rabbits with their natural predators—all in harmony and balance—men must now take on the job. No wonder we needed stories where Hehunn was no longer hunting within and with respect to nature, but controlling it, cutting it as the God Celi with a brutal scythe brought down a harvest or tested boys. I could see Celi's hands on the new plows that cut into the soil quickly, ruthlessly clearing the land for cultivation, and cutting a path through the months of gentler gods. Hehunn was becoming a god of cultivated hunts. I hoped Kutu's stories would not be lost, or this god would fade.

As I made my way to see Tages, I could not help but note

that it would soon be a bloody enough month without those hunters killed.

I skirted the long road that ran past Thefare's town and went all the way to the coast. I took to Jackal's Way, awed by the gleaming autumn canopy, even brighter with fall colors than my *reality* and a more vibrant smell of decay. I met Tages on the way. I saw him somehow, while I walked on my hidden path. I wasn't sure how I felt to speak with him again, but he was still my teacher. I stepped off that bright red carpeted road to the one of more browns and yellows and smelling more of rotting leaves.

He jumped at my sudden appearance and then shrugged. "Larce is looking for you," he said.

"I heard."

"As is Ravantha."

"I gathered that as well."

"You've been doing some good work in the villages. What have you learned?"

"Mentor, I have learned that I love the healing work we do, and I might wish for more study in divination, to be as good a Doctor-Diviner as you are," I said.

"I think you are on your way to moving beyond... divination. You found the books I left for you?"

"Yes," I said.

He gestured to an outcropping of rocks where a creek had bent toward the road. We sat down. I took fruit from my Tree and handed him one. He looked at it, cupping it in his hands, and brought it to his face and breathed its scent in deeply.

"I give you thanks," he said, then ate. He then looked at the book I'd handed him, but it was not one where he could examine pictures of plants I had drawn. It was all theory.

"These are my thoughts from the books you left me. You gave me a stack of dissertations among all the books. Thin pamphlets, rich with ideas, and thought-provoking."

"Aule sent them. They are papers researched by students, and written by the direction of their 'doctoral adviser,' as he calls his mentor now."

"One was a discussion of the World Tree. There are apparently many stories about it around the known world. One where it is a ladder to climb to see the path to the underworld, one where the shaman hangs from it and gains great wisdom at some cost."

"Yes."

"Another part of that dissertation reminded me of something Grandmother Turani said of another Tree—where man could not know what it suffers, because it's bitten or clawed above, one side rots, and it's gnawed from below."

"A man would only see the green." He chuckled. "*If* he can see it at all! Your Tree is all that as well, I believe, from what I've seen of your drawings. A Tree that is of the spirit world."

"Yes. I am thinking about that because you are holding and eating a fruit from a Tree you cannot see, but reveals—or could reveal—itself by the rocks you yourself have touched, rocks that its roots have displaced." I shivered in that moment, realizing that Grandmother Turani had left the child in the embrace of this Tree, giving it perhaps a more protected burial than otherwise. Perhaps I should have left my strange, secret *twin* there.

"You think this tree is the World Tree?" he asked, breaking into my pause.

I shook my head. "I think it is too young for that. It's daughter, perhaps?" I said, handing him another fruit. "It might be interesting to see if the seeds of this fruit would grow in your garden."

He smiled and nodded, putting it in his own bag. "You think these Trees might be related?"

"Yes. Worked with various *Bogeh*, shamans, or sangomas, or whatever other priestly names there are for those that do work similar to ours, thinking of the symbolism, I find it an interesting thought that there were so many stories where Trees—those trees bridge all the worlds in our living—the underworld, ours, and the divine in the sky."

"The Three Rivers in our craft: the White, the Red, and the Black."

"Yes."

The words made his face transform. He had had a sense of peace as he ate the fruit and talked. Now an unspoken distress grew on him, like the shadow of a rain cloud.

"What troubles you?" I asked.

"Ravantha and Thefare will have a battle in the coming days." He saw the look of dread on my face. "Not a big one," he assured me. "We are too *provincial*," he said, spitting out the word as if it were sour, "thank all the gods. It will be a display of ire, as if they were children needing to vent some displeasure instead of taking their bath."

"So... a tantrum, with sharp weapons."

"Yes. And there will be injury, some that will last the survivors the rest of their lives."

"You know so many people of influence. Could you not write someone and help stop this?"

"I did, and I fear, Sen of the Woods, that the influence even of a man in regular correspondence with authorities in

Jambrone's finest university is still a Doctor-Diviner. I might well be considered a *Witch Doctor* to the eyes of the nobility that rule the whole land. They do not seem to care about this provincial squabble. Thefare has no overlord, and Ravantha acknowledges no authority but her own."

I thought about the politics, and found it still just as confusing as ever. This part was clear.

"They have no power to give here," I said.

"Unless Thefare and Ravantha trespass beyond their borders. It makes no matter to them that I wrote. I've ignored their correspondence openly or by neglect. I'm paying for it now. For them, my title declares I'm a backwater quack in an area of the land considered far too rustic for their eyes. I am no spiritual leader of wisdom as in those stories once told in other lands, or even here."

I didn't say anything. His joy in studying alone had allowed the region to fall into a bit of chaos without him noticing, let his adept be threatened, and made the authorities think even less of him. I'm not sure if more frequent correspondence would have helped.

He went on. "Great chiefs and kings of the Tashihyel required the advice of their *Bogeh* before going to war." He threw the core of the fruit away to put his head in his hands.

After a brief pause where he hid his grief, he said, "That's what we should be, what we once were. The work we do that brings the divine to the nature of men, acknowledging our beloved dead—it is all fading. Our people do not want a myth or a Tree or even a person who reminds them of our connection to the past or the divine nature in all of us."

"The Tree is a symbol of how we are at the center of all

those things," I said.

I saw Jackal nearby and realized he'd been there all along, in his Way, listening. He was sitting, tongue out, with his patient grin. He put his paws forward in a stretch and then sat with his chest to the ground, his paws out before him. From his paws, the Way opened up and brought Tages into the realm with us.

I wondered what Tages would see, and waited.

I trembled, but thought back on what Tages had said. "Is Lord Aranthur one of those backwater lords?"

"No, and realizing how short my reach actually is, I begin to wonder how he ever thought to wed his son to Ravantha."

"For some reason, he wanted Thielle's necklace, and she was the closest likely maiden he could use to manipulate a *reasonable* trade. That is why Marce and Larce are here. Not for Ravantha's sake. Did you divine that none of them know anything about fighting in a war? How will it go?"

"Badly, and that is all to the good, for it will be a short battle." He paused and looked at me strangely. "I also know that one person will leave, never to return, and probably will pass into legend."

"Leave?" I asked.

"What is winter good for?" he asked.

"It lets seeds rest beneath the warm layer of decaying leaves and the layer of snow to build their strength for spring blow."

He nodded. "There is hidden power in winter. And the world has formed my apprentice till a winter's rest would make her more than her mentor ever will be."

And then he looked up and noticed Jackal's Way. He was trembling as he gazed into Jackal's amused eyes. There were tears in his eyes that did not fall.

"I don't know what you mean," I said.

Jackal laughed.

Tages shrugged. "I have no words to tell you. He might," he said, gesturing to Jackal. "Or that is possibly still on your path to learn."

I did not say anything. I had two reasons I wanted to leave. I merely did not know where that place would be, except north.

I felt overwhelmed. Too many disparate elements were in my reach, in my bag, or hands. A lost baby, a broken necklace, apples from a Tree only I could see, and Jackal sitting beside my mentor. And ever, Grandmother Turani's hope that I could somehow bind three things together before the Tree died. Jackal came near and rolled to show his belly.

"Do not trouble yourself," he said. "All of it put together is quite simple." He squirmed and rolled closer to Tages and me. "So simple that you will laugh when you see it."

I watched as Tages held his breath, but then reached down and rubbed Jackal's belly. Jackal then got up in an agile spin and nosed my bag.

"Give me one of your apples, Sen of the Woods, Sen from a Daughter Tree."

I handed him one. He held it in his mouth and ran off with his prize.

"I wish I understood what he said," Tages admitted.

"Respect from one teacher to another, I believe. As far as the lesson he gave, I do not understand it."

"Do not worry," Tages said. "The Way will open up to you. Clearly, you have a new and clever teacher, better than I could ever find. Now come. The fighting is north and west of here. It will come to the border of the Westvell villages.”

“Not down here?”

“Thefare is too canny not to see a threat and bring his men up this way. Ravantha has never experienced war, and threat only once. They will need us, as healers. Both sides.”

“Lead on,” I said.

“Take me to the ruins of the temple, please. It is closer to where the battle will be, I think, than my home. We can prepare ourselves for our work there as easily as in the field. I have brought what I have divined we will need.”

I nodded.

On the way back to Jammon’s temple, we spoke of various things. Jackal remained mostly with us, but saying nothing, leaving and returning at his own will.

“Did Velia, or you, come to harm because of the fire in the guard room?”

“No. They did not link her potion, or what they made of it, to be used on the guards. She was nowhere near the guards, or any that served them, tending to a bunch of nervous light-sleeping girls.”

“Good. I was worried when Larce told me what he’d done.”

Tages sighed. “He is a foolish man and will pay for his errors.”

“He nearly lost his arm.”

“He may lose more than that if he’s not careful. I believe I have divined some truth. Neither Thefare nor Ravantha will appreciate his actions, and he was foolish enough to err even more by letting some of his actions be revealed. If my insights with my divination are not in error, a much greater lord, and a much greater threat, looms over him.”

"I'm guessing Aranthur and all his fears and needs." I sighed and changed the subject. "Tell me of your work," I said. "I'm tired of thinking of all those people. I spent too much time just healing and long to hear more of what you have been studying without me. It's been nearly two months!"

"Not quite. Enough for people on both sides of the border to foment more stories about the evils of their neighbors. But as you wish, let us discuss our healing art."

After long discussions over letters, Tages had corrected his understanding of certain parts of the body. More, he'd found an interest in studying that went beyond what Vesalus had written in his books or in their correspondence. He made suppositions about air in lungs and our need for it, and the differences between arteries and veins based on the trick Gavius had shown me. He'd seen the lymphatic system, where illnesses often marked themselves under the chin or the armpit, becoming inflamed the way a boil might. Using his own observations as well as Ndeb's lore, he knew herbs that helped clean the body's blood and liver. In fact, among the things we grew in our garden were plants for healing certain ailments that Velia sold to the great city whenever her son would visit and could take them to market. Taking all these threads and putting them together, he had expanded on the study of the lymphatic system, and Vesalus had his work published in one of their great journals.

"I'm happy for you."

"It is an interesting system of healing. Even the breast tissue of a nursing mother has part of the lymphatic system, mingled in with the glands that bring nutrients to their young."

"If I remember correctly, there are other glands associated with the lymphatic system, including the spleen?"

"True."

Looking at his face, I saw his pride in his studies, yet he had had several blows to his reputation. The disregard he'd gotten from his attempts to stop this battle must have hurt. However much respect he had as a healer, it was yet more proof that the respect of the Doctor-Diviner's art was lessening. I had, this past year, been watching it happen. Though I was not to blame, I felt guilty that I was the one more often traveling the land. Working in his lab, in his study, he'd done incredible work, but had become forgotten. *He ought to go to Jambrone and the university: teach, study, learn. Gain the title of respect that he does indeed deserve*, I thought. I asked him instead, "So what errors did you uncover?"

"Well, Galen had only compounded errors of the past because his ideas were based on a study of pigs, sheep, or cows. No doubt the man knew quite a lot of the anatomy of pigs and cows, but little of the human body. He thought that those lymph vessels that work with the intestines drained into veins, and then into the liver."

"I take it that they don't?"

Tages went on. "It is my belief that it has far more to do with the immune system than with blood circulation. And how that works is a mystery. If Galen was wrong on so many things, maybe the heart doesn't create blood for the body to feed upon. So, I want to learn more of the lymphatic system, if I can."

"We know many plants that can aid the immune system," I said.

"And clean the blood."

We talked about various plants for the miles it took to get back to the ruins. I took him straight to the temple.

Tages still could not see the Tree. He saw the three

chimneys, the ruins of the altar—which, if it was Jammon's temple, probably meant a worktable, where the god or his people worked smithy work. But the Tree, with a few apples on it still, he could not see—even when Jackal brought him back into his Way.

"What does that mean?" I asked him.

"That it is a divine Tree. A Tree of the world."

"Like in legends and myths from the continent of the west? And hunter stories of Jackal, Deer, Lion, and Rabbit?" I asked.

He chuckled and said, "Yes. Indeed. Something tells me that you have more understanding of these stories than just words. And have for some time, or Jackal would not be so friendly and ask for an apple from you, and not steal it, as he no doubt could."

"Perhaps," I said, abashed.

He touched my arm and gave me a smile. "You have other teachers now than me. And this is good. As for this Tree, there are references to other trees like it all over, as you noted. Even here."

"Yes. The Milk Tree," I said.

"And if you were found at this Tree, it is your Milk Tree, and no other woman can claim you as their dependent. And you need answer to no man—except perhaps your mentor, for a little time more," he said, confirming what I'd already felt—even before I'd found the baby.

His words meant more than I had realized. I looked up at the Tree and reached up to get an apple that dropped into my hand as if it had been ready to fall. I handed it to Tages.

He sighed at the sight of fruit in his hand. Looking up at me, he bit into it. "It is good."

He had carried quite a lot with him. He'd brought our musical instruments, as well as herbs and paints. I was glad. My supply of paint was minimal. We painted ourselves and blessed the tools we would be using, including needle and thread. Tages had planned ahead. He'd brought glass vials for cleaned and sterile thread and needles. We also had knives and the means to make fire if we needed to cauterize wounds instead. We took our time, even while we felt the pressure to get to the upcoming battle.

One night, I took out the pieces of the broken necklace, except for what was sewn into the baby's clothes. I added yet more padding to the baby's bundle. I could not disturb her more. We were going into danger.

While Tages slept, I borrowed some of his tiny tools that were normally used to pull out arrow tips or large thorns, and such. I put the necklace back together. I could not put it together the way it had been, but I used the small chain links to make an added row with the remaining amber beads. So that I didn't have to take more gems off the baby's clothes, I set one of the two smaller pendants aside. To keep it safe, I put it on under my Doctor-Diviner robes and slept under the Tree. I dreamed.

Chapter Sixteen

There was a young woman in the front room of Grandmother Turani's stone house. It looked new. The walls were freshly plastered and painted with murals. Even in my dream, I yearned to look over them. I saw hints of a winged creature attending a familiar stylized Thielle. There was a hooded figure holding roses who walked with a flock of crows. Jackal was there, too, with a man who played with fire, Jammon perhaps. The style of paint was rough, the colors simple. The bordered patterns of paint were similar to what I'd seen on the walls of the women's compound. It was as if these drawings were much older, yet I could still trace out their meaning. My heart beat fast to think this.

My dreaming mind focused on the woman. She looked like a young Grandmother Turani. Her hair and eyes were much the same, though without the gray hair or the lines on her ancient face. She was far lovelier than anything I'd thought possible for any woman. This must be Thielle.

Above her head, was one open spot along the painted border of the entryway. A carving that I certainly hadn't noticed at Grandmother Turani's stone house—if it had been, time had worn it away.

Thielle smiled with content, gazing upon the cultured land that surrounded the area. Then she turned and left the stone house and walked on what was a familiar path to me now. She arrived at the Tree, which seemed to bow to her in greeting, and gave her something that gleamed amber in the light.

From the Tree's dying side came another woman. The Tree seemed to bow to her as well.

"Thielle," said the other woman, whose face was shadowed by the hood of her cloak. She lifted her hands, and the Tree bent down and seemed to drop something into them. It was not fruit. "I have the other half."

"Nhor, are you sure you want to do this?" Thielle asked. "The alchemist Jammon made this gift as a thing of beauty to celebrate his love, using skill and knowledge that are more than rare. He is near to the divine in this, in that embrace of knowledge the world is not ready for."

"It is a beautiful thing, but could never rival your beauty," said Nhor. "We could put it back together after he tore it apart. We are not the guardians of this thing. Still, he made it for you, before his love died."

"But he gave it to you. You should wear it."

Nhor said, "And then he broke it, and gave the pieces to me in his grief when all his alchemy could not save his beloved. I'm really not willing to wear it. Are you?"

Thielle shook her head, looking at the two parts of the necklace. Thielle took the shorter piece from Nhor's hand. The tree seemed to lower its branches toward their hands.

"Such love, such grief, on the shoulders of disease. Does the spirit of healing die by the sharp scalpel against the system of a body's workings?" Nhor asked.

"The world is not ready for the mingling of nature and science, beautiful though it is," Thielle said.

The Tree seemed to speak to them, bending branches down with fruit, one from each side, to the two women.

The two women each took part of the necklace. Thielle had the smaller piece. With parts of the necklace in hand, the two walked back to her painted grotto temple. There, she picked up a box quite familiar to me, Grandmother Turani's treasure box, and put it in there. "There, for when she'll find it."

"Do you think she'll find this part?" Nhor asked. "Do you really think she can? Or will?"

"Yes. And she'll bind it together again. But it will be new, and different, like the daughter of the World Tree in a different age that will come—and must come from the alchemy that rises from Jammon's work."

Nhor shook her head as she looked at her part of the damaged necklace. "I really hate it when things are misused. And this truly will be, as some will try to use her." Nhor shook her head. "Look what they've tried to make us to be—sisters divided, twins divided by jealousy, who are not bound to each other."

Thielle put her hand on her shoulder. "But you are more fearsome than fear. Things will be renewed, and healed."

"And you are of all things harmonious. Our time will soon be over. A new way of understanding what we were will overtake what legends about us obscured."

"People will one day learn what they did not have the

learning for when we were young! We were hints of what *could* be, and that is all. Is that not renewal and healing?"

"Yes, and it can only come when the time is ready," Nhor said. She looked around the stone house, with its gleaming frescoes. "You're going to be here an *exceptionally* long time," she said to her sister.

"Well, I'll have more freedom than you. You are burdened not only with hope but with being misunderstood and forgotten. I won't be stuck in some Ugly Grotto."

Nhor laughed. "And what's a stone house then?"

Thielle laughed as well. "Home."

"Sister, we must become forgotten for the next age to rise."

"And a new demigod to rise with it, bringing another way of understanding that might be lost in the lore Jammon works to inspire."

"Well, I must go," Nhor said. She stepped out into the garden that was lush, varied, and a glory compared to what I'd known, what an old woman and a young girl could tend with all of nature encroaching. A crow landed on Nhor's shoulder and pecked at the broken bit of necklace in her hands.

"You cannot have this bauble," she told her.

"It had better be lost in my nest," the Crow said. "For the mischief it will make."

Nhor shook her head. "And you a thing of nature!" she scolded. "It must have its natural time and a darkness that comes to all living things."

Crow shook his head in disgust and tried to grab it again with her sharp beak.

Chapter Seventeen

I woke, wondering what to make of the dream. I dared not think that Grandmother Turani had indeed been Thielle. But it had the same vision feel as the last one I'd had. A sense of truth. A knowledge firmer than a memory. I could not bear it.

I dared not discuss it with Tages to weigh the implications. I could only act with what I knew. I trembled and touched the necklace under my shirt. I did not want to defile a necklace once given to these goddesses with my all-too-human hands.

My hands trembled as I tried to undo the latch. I could not rip it off and break it further. Tages snorted, then groaned and woke. I dared not take it off now, under his observant eyes. I felt so ashamed of myself for my temerity in putting it on—even while I thought it would be safer than with the baby's bones.

I picked up apples that had fallen around me and gave one to Tages.

I noticed there was a gleam I'd not seen in his eyes for a

long time, and a bit more pepper in his gray hair than salt.

My stomach roiled in my tension, so I could not bring myself to eat one for breakfast. I prepared the altar for the last day's work. We created poultice and then wandered the outskirts and orchard for strong wood long enough for splints. I added that to my baggage, binding the sticks with rope, and added it to the pile of bags I would soon have to carry. Everywhere I went, even foraging for sticks or fresh herbs, I refused to leave my shoulder bag with the baby's bones behind.

On our last day there, Tages set up divination to see where we were first to go.

"North," he said. Slowly, he put away the symbols and set the threshing basket on the altar. "I'll leave this here," he said. He looked depressed. After a long moment, as he looked up toward a Tree he could not see, he asked, "What do we do, Sen, when we see sickness?"

"We remove the source of the illness. We either support the body by strengthening the immune system, or remove an infection that the body's defenses attempt to destroy."

"A thorn? Or splinter? Yes. Give me an example."

"Like that little boy Tudi, who had the splinter in his hand for months."

"Yes, I think I remember that. You tended him, if I recall."

"Yes, he was feverish, and his left armpit was swollen—your lymphatic system defending the body. I removed the thorn. I had to cut into the skin of his palm that had grown over it. Once the splinter was gone, Tudi's health improved rapidly. Such a small thing to make him so very sick," I said.

"Yes. Sometimes we do not believe small things are the sources of great harm or sickness—of a boy, a man, or even a woman."

I knew then that he was not speaking of a thorn.

"I would not call rape a small thing, or the loss of a child. Even if I am not that child."

"You've said that before. You have no proof."

"I do, Master," I said.

"Oh?"

"Yes. Ravantha told me that she had parts of Thielle's necklace from her rape. She'd sewn it into her baby's swaddling clothes." I shuddered again at the image.

"That's a horrible birth gift to give a child," Tages said.

"Yes, indeed," I said. "I found the baby under that Tree. Its bones are in my bag."

He shook his head, trying to hide his expression. He was as horrified as I could expect.

"Master, she was just left there. At least the animals didn't carry her off, scattering her bones. I'll carry her safely to a proper burial."

I wasn't sure I could explain this other part to him. I needed to carry my *sister*, my *twin*, to a burial that was more seemly than she'd had. Part of me could hardly bear to wonder why Grandmother Turani hadn't. The baby felt like a part of me I'd not known I'd lost. Only one other person had a greater claim.

"What do you intend to do with the baby?" He asked finally.

"Bury it... I think in a temple of Thielle so she can rest with love—or harmony, as you once reminded me—or a temple of Nhor, so she can rest with hope, and be guarded against evils of the tomb."

His face transformed with a smile. It showed me how

grieved he had been to discuss any of this, to admit this. "That is a good thought. You will have to do this after we tend to the wounded."

"Yes. I intend to," I said. I was so relieved that he trusted what I had and did not need to see the evidence.

"Sen, I think that if we are given an opportunity to heal the whole land by removing... its thorn, we should do so."

"What do you mean?"

"Divination is never so clear as to give us a plain path, but these things have sickened the whole land, and all we have done has not changed that. What we go to do now is only bind the surface ills, not what caused it," Tages said.

He paused. His face a map of deep contemplation that I could not read.

"It is not truly your job to mend this rift, but mine," he said finally.

"But can I not help?"

He shook his head, putting a hand on my arm. "No, Sen."

It was difficult for him to speak. I could see that it was taking more courage than him once admitting his inner sight, so valuable to a Doctor-Diviner, was fading. When he raised his head, and looked me in the eye, his voice was firm as he spoke.

"I must send you away to grow in your own Mastery. I have helped to cause this problem. I am the one who healed the cattle. Even if healing the cows gave Thefarland its formidable, but all-too-brief wealth. I did not fight to heal Ravantha further. I am the one who failed to guide Ravantha toward a path where she could find healing. I did not send Velia to care for her in her grief when she lost her child, as would have been right for them both. More, I am the one who ignored my own wife, so that she would work her grievance against me by winding you deeper into these troubles than ever before. I will not have you heal the wounds for which I am responsible. I must do the work or betray it—and it would be the last betrayal that would decimate the last honors lingering in our craft if I do not tend to our community."

He paused, taking my hands. "I would like to have you with me a little longer, but only by your choice," he said. "Come here, my dear."

He brought out the last of the paints and finished painting my face to show our office of work, since we could not go and do this work with masks. He then lifted my right hand gently. With his knife, he cut the Mastery symbol and then rubbed it with the healing white clay. He handed me a pot of sacred white clay that I could rub into it for the next few weeks.

"You are no longer my apprentice, no longer my adept, but my colleague," he said. He kissed my brow. In Ndeb, he said, "During the winter, you will be blessed not only by this scar, but by the blanket of white that builds the power of the seeds," he said. "You will be more than your master."

I trembled at this blessing. I could not believe him.

With that, we headed toward the battle that was to come.

E • N • D

About the Author

Mab Morris lives in Dahlonega, Georgia, with a number of cats and a Celtic labyrinth of her own design. Her storytelling and her love of fantasy began at a very young age, where she was drawn to Ursula K. Le Guin and J.R.R. Tolkien. Mythology, history, and folklore are her passion.

She writes mystical fantasy books set in the past, present and future of the world of Ihyel, where demi-gods and mortals alike struggle with their fate. She also writes the murder-mysteries of The Bone Reader, about Cemirowl who speaks with the dead, and the Regency adventures of gender-fluid spy Alex Goodward.

Check out www.mabmorris.com for more info.

Other Books by Mab Morris

Lost Bones

Book One of The Bone Reader

Cemirowl is gifted, and cursed. She sees the spirits of the dead, and sees the future in her basket of bones; her sight is cryptic, lacking, and mostly useless. In her tiny village, she is a priestess, but still an object of curiosity and an outcast.

A chance meeting brings one of the king's caballiers to her door for a reading, for nothing more than some entertainment. He is well-entertained indeed by her predictions of his lady loves... and far less so when she foretells a coming death. He leaves, dismissing her. But for all that her power is mysterious and often confusing, it is never, ever wrong.

When Queen Tidyri is murdered, the caballiers return for Cemirowl. She is brought unwillingly into the palace and into a web of intrigue and lies, where King Larthor rages in his grief. He demands that Cemirowl now use her gifts to find the one who killed his beloved wife.

Cemirowl must draw on all her abilities – her powers, no matter how unreliable; her intuition for reading people; her knowledge; and her wits – to discover the murderer, lay the spirits of the dead to rest, and help the living to grieve and find peace. And, perhaps, she will finally find a place where she belongs.

LOST BONES is a fantastical murder mystery set in the rich world of Ihyel, where the hard-won peace between two kingdoms rests on the shoulders of one determined, compassionate priestess.

Fate of the Red Queen

A Standalone Novel in the World of Ihyel

"I am not defeated! If my body falls, it is only that alone which dies!"

Faced with a war she could not win, the Red Queen sealed her country's fate with her final sacrificial pledge. Yezgyin was locked into undeath, the people and their enemies alike cursed to neither live nor die unless the spell could one day be broken.

Centuries passed, and history faded into legend. Kuen, a newly anointed Red Nun, escapes a vicious attack on her convent, and flees into the Jungle of the Dead. Amid the ruins of lost Yezgyin, she mourns the death of her mentor and all she has known, utterly lost to her grief. But the jungle whispers of her, and its otherworldly inhabitants welcome her as their new Red Queen, the one who will break their curse.

Kuen must find her way through the demands of the past and the hopes of the future, as the Red Queen's ancient adversary returns to win the war that never ended. With the life and death of Yezgyin at stake, she must fight for her own fate, or she and the people of the Jungle will never truly live again.

FATE OF THE RED QUEEN is a standalone novel set in the mysterious world of Ihyel.